COOPER AND PACKRAT

Mystery of the Lost Lynx

"Get lost" in a good book!

Tamra Wight

By Tamra Wight

Illustrations by Carl DiRocco

P.O. Box 10
Yarmouth, Maine 04096
www.islandportpress.com
info@islandportpress.com

Print ISBN: 978-1-952143-36-6
Ebook ISBN: 978-1-952143-38-0
Library of Congress Control Number: 2021946863

Printed in the United States of America

Dean L. Lunt, Editor-in-Chief | Publisher
Piper K. Wilber, Assistant Editor
Trevor Roberson, Book Designer

Dedicated to:
Game wardens, biologists, gamekeepers,
and wildlife rehabilitators everywhere—thank you
for all you do to protect our precious wildlife.

And to Melissa K., my editor, my cheerleader,
my friend. I'm so happy you tagged along
on this adventure.

Chapter 1

A female lynx gives birth to a litter of one to five kittens, each one weighing only seven ounces at birth.

I slid my hands one at a time into my blue winter gloves, then stuffed them into my red down jacket pockets as deep as they would go. Tucking my chin into the scarf wrapped around my neck, I stomped the snow under my boots, packing it down. Turning in a circle on the ice, I scanned the frozen-over Pine Lake.

Back around Christmas, Dad had drilled a hole in the ice and declared the lake ready for winter activities. According to Warden Kate, our local game warden and my wildlife mentor, you only needed the ice to be four inches thick to walk on it safely. But Dad liked to find at least eight before he'd let my little sister Molly and me go out on it. Mom needed to see a gazillion inches. No, more like a gazillion times eight inches.

Until yesterday, we hadn't had any snow. But late last night a nor'easter dumped over a foot and a half of the fluffy white stuff. It'd given us a snow day, and better yet, a day off from school right before February vacation break. The best kind!

"It's gonna warm up to thirty degrees tomorrow." Packrat reached up to his lined, brown bomber hat which covered his shaggy brown hair and tugged the side flaps down over his ears.

Summer laughed, making the purple pom-pom on her knitted yellow hat bob back and forth. "A real heat wave!"

Roy snorted, his warm breath hitting the cold air like a puff of steam. Using a metal skimmer with a long skinny handle, he lifted ice chunks and slivers from our fishing hole in the ice. He wasn't as big a fan of winter as the rest of us. Ice-fishing and snowmobiling could get him to join us, but building a snowman? Not so much.

Packrat opened his long, tan trench coat with its many pockets. Taking off one of his gloves, he reached inside a long skinny pocket to pull out a two-foot-long fishing pole before buttoning up his coat again.

The minute he and his mom, Stacey, had found out school was canceled this morning, they'd left Weld and arrived here at my family's campground to stay the week. An hour later, Roy's dad had driven him up from Portland to drop him off.

As soon as they'd gotten here, Packrat, Roy, and I had loaded all our ice-fishing gear onto a sled. Roy towed the sled behind his black ATV to the lake's edge and then we pulled the sled out onto the ice to our favorite winter fishing spot. We knew it would have six feet of water under the ice as well as plant life on the lake floor, making it the perfect location to fish for bass. Summer had spied us from her house across the way and joined us within twenty minutes.

Right now, we were the only ones out here. It felt pretty cool to have the two-hundred-acre lake all to ourselves.

"We're getting more snow tonight!" Summer rubbed her mitten-covered hands together like my little sister Molly did whenever Dad said, "Let's go get ice cream." I shot Summer a grin. She smiled back shyly.

Packrat held his fishing hook in one hand, and a tiny minnow in another. He made an I'm-so-sorry kind of face to the minnow like he always did when he put bait on a hook. Adjusting the weighted sinker above the hook that would take the minnow to the lake floor, he tossed it in the fishing hole before it froze. "Good thing! We're gonna need a lot more snow if we want to build a snow fort and sleep out in it."

"Or snowshoe to the other end of the lake," said Summer.

"Or have a snowball fight," Roy added.

I shuddered, thinking about being the target of one of Roy's fastballs. I got off the subject faster than he could throw.

"I almost forgot," I said. "I talked to Dad this morning, and he agrees Monday is the best day to have our fishing derby for the campers. I just have to check in with Warden Kate."

The derby was one of many events at our campground's winter festival, planned for next week.

"Cool!" Roy put his bare hands in his armpits. Giving us a slanted grin, he said, "How about a little fishing bet? Just between us."

Summer, Packrat, and I groaned. Betting was Roy's thing, though, so he didn't pay any attention to us. He kept right on talking.

"The one with the smallest fish at the end of the derby has to take a polar plunge."

"Polar plunge?" Packrat waggled his fishing pole, so the line jiggled in the hole. We couldn't see it, but the tiny minnow at the end of his line bounced along the lake floor every time Packrat moved it. Hopefully, there was a big, fat lake trout or bass getting curious down there. "There's no open water to jump in. It's not like you can drill a hole and dunk us like bait."

Roy shrugged. "Fine. Then what if the losers cook all the keeper fish for the winner? They have to treat him like a king!"

Summer laughed. "That's doable. I can't fish because I promised Cooper I'd be scorekeeper for the derby. But I'd love to be there when you cook and serve supper to King Cooper." Summer winked at me. I felt my ears turning red, and not from the cold.

Roy frowned. "You always bet on Cooper lately. I think you—"

"Hey!" Summer cut Roy off to point across the lake at an undeveloped chunk of woods. "What's that?"

Something—two somethings, actually—were traveling through the woods on a snowmobile trail. Long and low to the ground, they looked

an inch tall from here, but moved faster than someone snowshoeing or cross-country skiing.

Packrat dug into one of the many outer pockets he had in his trench coat. Pulling out binoculars, he lifted them to his eyes. "Whoa! Those are dogsleds!" he said, before handing the binoculars to me.

"Cool!" Summer bounced on her toes and held out a hand. "Can I see?"

Just then, the drone of a moving machine filled the air. Scanning the lake, I saw a yellow snowmobile flying across the ice parallel to the dogsleds.

My eyes went back and forth between them, watching the snowmobile coming up fast and furious, gaining on the sleds.

"Good thing they aren't on the same trail," Packrat said.

Right then, the dogsleds turned to come out on the ice, heading toward us.

The snowmobile didn't slow down. Instead, it seemed to speed up!

"They don't see it!" Summer's voice rose.

We were so far away we couldn't warn them. We could only hold our breath and wait.

At the last minute, the snowmobile sped up to race across the path of the dogsledders, missing them by what looked to us like inches.

"Someone ought to take that driver's sled away," Roy complained. "Drivers like them give snowmobilers like me a bad reputation."

I saw one of the dogsledders raise an arm in the air.

"They aren't happy," Summer said, passing the binoculars back to me.

The sleds traveled straight across the lake toward us now, and the closer they got, the more detail I could see. Each long, wooden sled had six dogs in harnesses pulling it. One rider stood on the back of each sled, holding on. The only sound from the dogs was panting, their breath creating fog in the cold air. I swear every face wore a smile.

I remembered something Mom had said last night, but at the time I'd only heard blah-blah-blah because I'd been making a to-do list for our winter festival.

"You know," I told my friends, "I think they're staying with us! At the campground!"

"Dogsledding." Roy made a what-the-heck face.

I lowered the binoculars, confused. My friend liked to move fast, choosing motorboats over kayaks and dirt bikes over hiking. But dogsledding could be fast and fun and dangerous.

I opened my mouth to say so, but Packrat's hushed voice came first.

"Umm, guys?" he whispered. "Turn around real slow."

Back on the lakefront, right where our dock would normally be in the summer months, a large wildcat stepped out of the woods and onto the ice.

"Oh!" cried Summer. "It's so beautiful! I've never seen a cat like that before!"

"*Shhhh!*" I warned, while Roy snickered and Packrat rolled his eyes.

"Sorry," she whispered, tucking a strand of brownish-blonde hair behind her ear and making a zipping-her-lips motion with her free hand. Her green eyes sparkled with excitement.

Just a few feet onto the lake, the cat turned back to face where it had come from.

Right away, I noticed it had a stub of a tail, with the tip looking as if it'd been dipped in black paint.

"Bobcat?" whispered Roy.

I shook my head. The cat's fur was grayish with black markings and white frosted tips. It stood one and a half feet tall, with long legs and really, really big, furry paws.

"See the black tufts of hair standing straight up from the tips of its ears, making them look even more pointy?" I whispered. "And how there's a beard on either side of its chin coming down to a point? Those markings make it a lynx."

"Whoa!" Packrat took his binoculars back from me and put them to his eyes. "I've never seen one before!"

The lynx walked backward a couple of steps. It looked tense, like it wanted to stay, but also ready to bolt in a heartbeat at the slightest sense of danger.

Two more lynx stepped out of the tree line, side by side, slowly stalking the first.

Summer sucked in a breath. Even Roy gasped.

"Whoa," Packrat whispered again. These two were at least half a foot bigger. Every time they took a couple slow steps forward, the little one went backward.

Raaaaaar! Raaaaaaaaar! the biggest of the three yelled. Immediately, its partner repeated the call. Back and forth they went, tag-teaming. The calls were eerie, creepy, starting low and rising to a high-pitched cat yowl. You could almost hear words in those cries, and this was not a hey-nice-to-see-you-again kind of meeting.

"Cooper!" Summer cried, forgetting her promise to be quiet. "What's happening? Is that their kit?"

Raaaaaar!

"It's called a kitten. And I don't know."

The little lynx crouched low, still stepping backward very, very slowly. Raaar! It tried to answer, but sounded unsure. The largest lynx rushed forward, stopped in its tracks, and head-butted the little one.

I tried to remember my lynx facts.

"It's almost mating season; maybe they're shooing last year's kitten off their territory."

"*Raaaaaaar!*"

I didn't know what the bigger lynx said, but this time the little one scrambled backward before turning to race across the beach area in front of us, and into the woods.

The pair of lynx hollered again in an and-stay-gone-too kind of way, before stepping back into the tree line.

"Wow!" I cried. "I've never seen anything like it! I've never even seen a lynx before—and there were three! And they were hollering!"

Packrat lowered his binoculars, and I noticed for the first time, his brows were furrowed. "I can't be a hundred percent sure, but the little lynx?" He turned to look at me.

"Yeah?"

"It might have had a black collar."

What? No. No way. It was illegal to have a pet lynx here in the state of Maine.

"Like a loon has a white-collar marking? The lynx had a mark on its fur?"

"No." Packrat's worried eyes met mine. "More like a pet collar."

Chapter 2

Lynx use their nose, ears, and eyes to communicate.
They also use their voices.

A snowball whizzed by my head, followed by the sound of giggling. Summer!

I grinned, and my heart beat a little faster, mostly from the snowball almost pelting me. But also because these last couple of months, something had shifted between Summer and me. Oh, we were still friends and all. We both liked ice-fishing and wildlife and being outdoors. But lately, I thought a lot about her when we weren't together, wondering where she was and what she was doing, for no reason at all! I'd almost asked Packrat and Roy about it, but I'd chickened out. What the heck was wrong with me?

Bending down, I gathered a bunch of last night's wet snow in my gloves and quickly formed a snowball to launch back at her. She ducked behind a tree.

Within seconds, I'd unloaded two more snowballs at Packrat. The first missed by a mile, but the second hit him square in the chest, and my crazy friend pretended to stumble backwards, falling in a heap, a hand over his heart.

"You got me!" he groaned.

Laughing, I bent to gather more snow into balls to rearm myself. And there was plenty of it! Just like Summer had predicted, we'd gotten two feet of the wet kind overnight. Dad was out plowing, and my friends and I had started shoveling off the store porch. One of us had thrown a snowball, and suddenly we found ourselves in an all-out snowball war!

A gasp and another giggle made me glance up. Roy stood gleefully, ten feet away, a humongous rectangular-shaped snowball in his hands over his head. I groaned. I knew from experience that he'd picked up that chunk from the piles of snow Dad's plow had tossed to the sides of the road. My friends and I called them frozen-neck-makers because once they hit your head, they broke into a gazillion pieces and at least one chunk would find its way onto your neck inside your coat. Or worse, slip inside your shirt onto bare skin, leaving a long cold trail as it melted down, down, down!

"Nooooooo!" I hollered, shivering at the thought.

I jumped up to make a run for it. My left boot slipped on an ice patch, and I wobbled. Throwing a hand to the ground to steady myself, I squished my last snowball flat.

Roy laughed slowly. Evilly. Taking two steps toward me, I could tell he loved my panic. My friend was enjoying the hunt.

I grabbed my coat collar with both hands and tightened it around my neck against the Roy-made avalanche that would soon turn me into a human snowman.

A snowball whizzed over my right shoulder, hitting bare skin on Roy's left wrist between his glove and his coat sleeve. He jumped in surprise, his hand automatically shaking the cold snow off. The weight of the frozen-neck-maker now balanced awkwardly in his right hand, throwing him off balance. Back and forth Roy wobbled, trying to gain control, until . . . the frozen-neck-maker plopped on Roy's own head.

I sucked in a breath, standing up quickly. "Now Roy, stay calm—"

Summer put a mittened hand to her mouth and snorted into it.

Packrat, the peacemaker, moved toward Roy with a hand out to brush the snow off him, but stopped at the look on Roy's face.

Roy stood perfectly still. The only thing left from the gigantic mound of snow he'd held was a little snowball balancing on his head. Roy's mouth formed into a big "O."

No one—*no one*—hit Roy with a snowball without permission and got away with it, except, of course, Summer, Packrat, and me.

But none of us had thrown it.

"You had it coming" came a voice over my right shoulder.

A girl with long, blue-tipped black hair stepped up beside me, rubbing her gloved hands together to brush the snow off. A half-smile formed as she tipped her head to the side. "Three against one? And you want to drop an iceberg on his head?"

I laughed at the picture in my mind of a Hercules-like Roy with an iceberg held high. I choked it back quickly with a cough when Roy didn't smile, too.

"Thanks," I quickly said to the girl. "But these guys are my friends. We were just, you know, messing around."

"I always drop icebergs on his head," Roy muttered. "It's not my fault he's no good at snowball fights."

The girl lifted one eyebrow and stared coolly at Roy.

Instantly, Roy straightened his shoulders and lifted his chin to stare coolly back.

Oh boy.

Getting a good look at my rescuer now, I could see she was older than us by a couple of years. Her winter boots, hat, and coat were black with a blue stripe. Everything matched, almost like a uniform.

Summer stepped toward her. "I know you! You were driving the dogsled yesterday!" She was talking so fast her purple pom-pom was dancing.

The girl snapped her fingers. "Right! And you four were ice-fishing."

Summer's sparkling eyes told me an avalanche of questions was about to drop on the girl.

"Are you camping here? Are the dogs yours? Where are they now? Or did you just hire the ride? No, that can't be, because you were on the back, driving it. How do you get the dogs to go? How do you get them to stop? And—"

"Summer!" Packrat exclaimed, "Geez! You're embarrassing us! She—"

The black-haired girl raised a gloved fist. Packrat leaned backward.

I frowned, sidestepping toward Summer. What the heck?

The girl's thumb popped up out of the fist. "I'm camping here for the week, just got in yesterday." Her pointer finger went up. "The dogs are mine and my mom's." A third finger went up. "They're back at the campsite resting, Mom and I took a daybreak run, hoping to tire them out so they wouldn't bark so much and bug other campers." A ring finger joined the rest. "I get them to pull by saying, 'Let's go.'" By the time her pinky finger went up, Summer, Packrat, and I were smiling. "Stop is 'Whoa.'"

Roy was not smiling. Crossing his arms, he harrumphed.

Summer bounced on her heels. "Can we meet them?"

The girl shrugged. "Sure."

"Geez." Roy rolled his eyes and folded his arms. "Got a name?"

"The dogs?"

I knew that she knew Roy didn't mean the dogs. She was good. Really good.

Again, the two had a staring match. Packrat, Summer, and I shared a look through the heavy silence of it all.

Roy unfolded his arms to kick a small snowball out of the road, back into the plowed pile beside it. "Your name."

"It's Wynter. With a 'y.'"

"You're kidding!" Summer's eyes lit up even more. "You'll never guess what my na—"

Roy burst out laughing, cutting her off. "No way! You've got to be joking!"

Summer put her hands on her hips and glared at him.

I shoved his shoulder. "C'mon, cut it out!"

"Yeah," Packrat chimed in. "You're being rude, even for you."

Roy wiped his eyes. "She runs a dogsled. And her name is Wynter!"

Any other kid camper would have stomped away, punched him out, or cried. This girl didn't do any of those things.

"You think my first name is funny?" she asked. When Roy nodded, Wynter flicked the hair on the right side of her face back over her shoulder. "Wait until you hear my middle name."

Roy grinned from ear to ear. "What is it? Flake?"

"Ha! Not even close." The girl tucked her hands deep in her pockets and tipped her head to the side as she studied Roy. "And I'll bet you can't guess it. How about a friendly wager?" A big, bright, blinding smile flashed across Wynter's face. "You guess my middle name in five guesses, you win. If you can't get it in five tries, I win. And the loser—that'll be you, of course—has to be a human target for one hundred snowballs."

Chapter 3

Adult lynx have no predators, but kittens are prey to wolves, hawks, eagles, and owls.

Summer begged to meet the dogs right then and there. Wynter agreed, and before I knew it, we were all following her eagerly toward her campsite. Well, Summer, Packrat, and I were. Roy followed about twenty feet behind, kicking snowballs off the plowed dirt road, hands deep in his pants pockets, muttering something about wasting good snowmobiling daylight.

I studied the campsites nestled among the woods as we walked down the camp road. Normally my family's business, Wilder Family Campground, would be sleeping under a blanket of untouched snow this time of year. The only people who lived here in the winter were my mom, dad, my little sister Molly, and me. And of course, the wildlife who came out to hunt and play in and around the sites and buildings after our campers packed up and left in the fall.

This winter, though, my family was trying something new: a winter festival during February school break! I'd planned it all after watching Packrat and Roy leave last fall. Oh, Mom and Dad didn't say yes right away to bringing in a few winter campers for the week. In fact, I got a resounding "No" at first. So, I researched and reported back on their arguments, like how campers deal without having water at the campsites. I kept bugging them, listing all the cool winter activities we could offer.

Then, when I got Mom on my side by mentioning a fishing derby, she ran the numbers and told Dad we'd actually make a little money. He'd grumbled and warned us, "You'll have to run this place all on your own, because I'm going to a campground owners' conference that week." After that, we reeled him in to our plan like a fighting trout on a lure.

"How many dogs do you have?" Summer's bouncy, enthusiastic voice brought me back to today. Rounding the corner onto Wynter's camp road, we could hear barks ranging from deep and booming to high and shrill.

"We only have thirty total," Wynter answered, like it was no big deal. Didn't everybody have thirty dogs? Packrat whistled low. Wynter added, "This trip, we brought twelve. Six for each sled."

We turned the corner, our heavy winter boots crunching on the frozen dirt road. Way down at the end, I could make out her dogs pulling on the ropes which kept them on the campsite. If they weren't tied to their stakes, I had no doubt they would have swarmed us like bees.

Mom and Dad had picked a great campsite for them. Big and flat, and at the very end of this dead-end street with no one on either side or behind, it gave Wynter and her mom plenty of room to spread out.

Dad had pushed the snow well off the back of their site, and cleared the site to the right of it, too. With all the other campsites on this street still covered in the heavy, wet stuff, Wynter and her mom looked like they were wilderness camping in the middle of the Maine woods. They had a twenty-foot trailer parked off to the right which they'd towed in with a big, black four-door pickup truck. In the bed of the pickup sat a white truck camper. No, wait. It was a truck camper for the dogs! There were six little doors on either side, three on the bottom, three on top. Each door had a small window.

Packrat looked inside one of the windows. "Your dogs travel in style!"

"Each dog has their own cubby," Wynter explained, "and we lay straw inside to help them stay warm."

Wynter whistled two short calls. The dogs sat but kept barking. Not a get-off-my-site bark, more like dog-talk. Tails wagging, tongues hanging out, butts wiggling.

"Well trained!" I was impressed.

We stepped onto the campsite and Wynter greeted each of the dogs with a look or a quick mittened pat on the head. Right away, I noticed two different breeds.

"These six are my dogs," Wynter said. I could hear the pride in her voice. "They're Chinooks."

"Chinooks?" I asked, thinking they looked a lot like long-legged Labs.

"I've never heard of them," Packrat said, reaching out to pat a dog with red fur and tall pointy ears.

"They almost went extinct," Wynter explained. "But there are a few breeders who are trying to help them make a comeback. We're one of them. I help out with chores around our kennel and with dogsled training, but I don't get paid, so sometimes I get the pick of a litter for my own team."

She pointed to the dog Packrat was petting.

"That's Fox, the first pup I ever trained. The white one over there? His name is Wolf. The goofy guy with one ear up and one hanging halfway down like a helicopter," Wynter said, shooting the dark brown dog a grin, "is Moose. Behind him are Grizzly and Bear. They're brothers." If Wynter hadn't told me Grizzly and Bear were Chinooks, I might have mistaken their faces for German shepherds because of the dark markings on their floppy ears.

Wynter smiled softly down at a black dog, the only one in the team of six who wasn't excitedly barking at having visitors.

"And this is Raven, my favorite lead dog." Raven's black eyes, with tan spots at the inner corners, gave her a face full of expression. Raven watched, taking everything in. And she seemed as curious about us as we were about her.

I got down on one knee to pat the side of her neck and shoulder.

"What about the other team?" Summer asked. "I love how furry they are, and how their tails curl up onto their backs!" She walked over to pat a white female with red on either side of her face and a white line from her nose to her forehead. "What breed are they?"

"That's my mom's team, all Canadian Eskimo dogs, and wicked smart, too. You're petting River. The all gray one with white socks over there is Sky. The tan female is named Star because of the white mark on her forehead. Comet is the black-and-white male. Mom named him because of the streak of white from his nose to the back of his head. Aurora got her name because the gray fur on her back looks like it's dripping down her white sides. And then there's Blizzard."

When Wynter said his name, the pure white dog hopped up to dance in a circle on all four feet, tugging at his rope. He wore a huge smile, eyes twinkling, trying to get at Summer.

"Okay, okay," she told him between giggles. "I'm coming!"

Roy, who'd been standing all this time with his hands in his pockets just outside the circle of dogs, gave one short laugh. "Blizzard? Really? Hey, ever lose him in a storm?"

Standing up, Wynter explained. "Naming our pups is a big deal for us. First, we pick a theme. My team's theme is Canadian animals. Mom's is what she loves most about Canada." She looked coolly at Roy. "My family takes naming very, very seriously."

I could tell the wheels were turning in Roy's brain. "Aha! So, your middle name goes with your first name!" he exclaimed. "Your middle name is Storm! Wynter Storm!"

Wynter laughed. "Good one, but no. One guess down, four to go!"

Roy picked up a foot-long stick from the ground, muttering to himself about only having five guesses. Several of the dogs jumped up, pulling at their ropes, trying to get to him. Roy's right arm went up and back, and he leaned onto his right foot to hurl the stick into the woods.

Moose fell to all fours, pulled his rope tight, gave a shake of his head, and slipped free! Eyes only on Roy, he bounded toward my unsuspecting friend at breakneck speed!

Chapter 4

The print size of a full-grown lynx is the same size as a mountain lion.

It all happened in slow motion.

"Look out!" I hollered a warning to Roy. What would Moose do to him?

Roy looked back at us, the stick still in his hand above his shoulder. Moose launched himself full force into the air, all four feet off the ground, snow spraying everywhere. His mouth was wide open, showing a perfect set of sharp canine teeth.

Roy's eyes widened and his mouth made an O shape.

Moose grabbed the stick in his mouth right before he plowed into Roy's side with both front feet. The two of them went down in a heap, a tangle of arms and legs, hands and paws.

Roy rolled around, trying to get Moose off of him. Finally, the dog stood and planted both paws square on Roy's chest. Looking my friend in the eye, Moose dropped the stick on Roy's chest and barked, once, twice, three times.

"Wynter? *Wynter*!" Roy's arms were over his face. "WYNTER!"

Wynter calmly approached. Scratching Moose under the chin, she cooed, "Did you get the bad boy's stick? Did you? Good Moose!"

Summer chuckle-coughed. Packrat snorted. I held my breath.

Moose backed off Roy, but his rear end wiggled in excitement as he kept his eyes glued to him.

Roy didn't exactly look scared as he crawled backward before standing to rub snow off himself. But he didn't exactly look like he was having much fun, either.

"It's the stick," Wynter explained. "Moose would plow through a wall of people—heck, he actually did plow through a wooden fence once—to fetch a stick or a ball!"

Roy bent to pick up the stick. "A little warning woulda been nice," he grunted.

Moose barked loudly until Roy heaved the stick down the road.

The dog took off, tearing after it. Bringing the stick back, he dropped it on Roy's boots and barked as if to say, *More! More!*

I saw a tiny, crooked smile etch upward on Roy's face before he picked up the stick to toss it again.

"Imagine," I said, surveying the scene around me. "Twelve dogs. My mom won't even let me have one!"

Raven nudged my thigh with her nose. As I glanced down, she looked up at me with thoughtful eyes. "Raven's wicked calm compared to the others."

"That's partly why she's my lead dog," Wynter said. "She's smart, fast, and patient. She listens well, and I could trust her in any situation. If a squirrel runs across the trail, she doesn't bat an eye, and she wouldn't let any of the other dogs, either." She gently stroked Raven from the back of her ears, down her neck. "She trusts me, and I trust her."

Wynter smiled at me over Raven. I smiled back.

Summer moved between us to put a hand on my arm. She gave me a silent look, and before I could ask what was wrong, she pointed down.

About five feet away in the snow, behind the truck, was a paw print. It seemed a touch smaller than a men's medium-sized glove. I counted four toe pads and a center foot pad.

I followed the prints to the edge of the campsite, where the tracks went into newly fallen snow, heading for the woods.

Raven sniffed the tracks, and the hair on the back of her neck went up.

"The dogs got a little restless in the middle of the night, last night," Wynter said, looking thoughtfully at the tracks.

"Do they stay outside?" Roy asked from behind us.

"No, we put them in their crates." She pointed to the truck camper. "They have straw to sleep on, and they're locked up safe."

I scrunched down to look closer. Summer practically had her chin on my shoulder, as she leaned in to ask, "Fox?"

"Too small," Wynter and I said at the same time.

We shared another smile. She knew her tracks.

"Coyote?" Roy asked. "Attracted to the dogs?"

Wynter shot him a quick look.

"Bobcat?" Packrat guessed.

I shook my head at all of them.

"See how the paw prints are close together? And how they don't sink all the way to the bottom of the snow? Almost like they're floating. And here." I used my pointer finger to outline the overall ice-cream-cone shape, ending at the top of the print, where it looked like the snow had been kicked forward. "The animal isn't sinking into the snow; it's walking mostly on top. Its paws are like snowshoes."

I glanced up at Wynter. "You had a lynx come through here last night. A young one, too."

Chapter 5

Lynx use thoroughfares for travel,
especially in the winter.

"Lynx!" Wynter said the word in one slow breath as her eyes followed the trail of tracks into the woods. "It must have been curious about the dogs."

I raised an eyebrow. Not everyone knew how curious lynx could be.

Summer slipped in between us again, tipping her head to look up at me. "Do you think it's one of the lynx we saw yesterday?"

I wondered the same thing. These tracks looked smaller than some I'd seen before. "Maybe it's the younger of the three?"

Packrat caught my eye, and I knew he was thinking about the strange collar it had been wearing. "Lynx are curious, but still—"

"They don't usually come close to people or other animals." Wynter finished for me. "It would have watched from the shadows and safety of the trees."

Packrat pulled his phone from an inside jacket pocket. Crouching down, he took close-up photos of the prints next to his glove for a size comparison. "I'll take these pictures in case we find more tracks and want to compare," he explained.

Wynter glanced toward her dogs. "You saw three lynx? That sure is a lot in one territory."

"I've been thinking about that," I told her. "If two of them were pairing up to mate, they might have teamed up to chase the little one off."

Roy was petting Moose with one hand, not looking at any of us. I wasn't sure he was even listening until he chimed in. "Still, I'd put these pups in their dog boxes when you aren't around."

Wynter whirled on him, hands on hips. "Are you trying to scare me?"

Roy's eyes hardened in response. "I just wanted to give some advice. Geez. Don't make such a big deal about it."

Wynter flicked back a lock of hair. "Mom and I enter dogsled races and sometimes camp out in the wild. Still, these dogs aren't working dogs. They're family! We raised each one from a puppy. I'd never put one in danger."

Roy's eyes went from annoyed to curious. "You race?"

Aha! Finally! Something to get my old friend to lay off our new friend. Not surprising that of everything she'd said this morning, the word race was the one thing that got his attention.

"Yeah." Wynter gave us a follow-me look as she weaved her way through the dogs with them dancing in place, barking, looking for attention.

In front of her camping trailer sat two wooden sleds shaped like baby cradles on skis. We gathered around the first one. It had a small, square deck on the back where a person could stand while holding onto the handle as a team of dogs pulled them along. The sled had room for one person to sit with some gear.

Roy scoffed. "*This* is what you race in? It looks like it'd fall apart the first time you hit a speed bump. *Pffft!* I'd take my snowmobile any day."

Summer rolled her eyes. "Oh, come on, Roy! You know you want to try it." She glanced shyly at Wynter. "I know I want to."

Wynter smiled at her. "We'll find time to make it happen."

Feeling something wet touch the palm of my hand, I looked down to find Raven, her nose inches from my hand. Looking from me to the sled and back at me again. Wynter laughed. "You found a friend! She wants you to go for a ride, too!"

I crouched down. The second my nails hit the scratching spot behind Raven's left ear, her eyes closed slightly and her tongue lolled out. A smile curved upward. She looked so relaxed, so happy, like I was giving her a full body massage.

"Oh!" Packrat's hands went to the top of his bomber hat. He pointed to Wynter. "I wonder if—"

"Yeah!" I knew exactly what he was thinking! "Dogsled rides!"

Wynter's head whipped back and forth between us as we tag-teamed her.

"Are you and your mom gonna camp here all week?" I asked.

Say yes, say yes, say yes!

"We have a winter festival happening right here," Packrat explained.

I jumped in. "Maybe you and your mom could give rides? To the other campers?"

Summer went up on her toes in excitement, clapping her mittened hands together. "I bet everyone would love to learn about the dogs and everything!"

"You could charge a fee," I suggested.

Mom and Dad had taught me too well. I figured running the dogs had to cost something, after all, like for their food.

Roy kicked a snowball, rolling it toward the group of dogs. Wolf pounced on it. Plopping to the ground with the snowball between his paws, he began chomping on it. "I guess a ride from one end of the lake to the other would be a good run and all," Roy said. "But what about snowmobile rides? That'd be fun, too!"

Fox pulled her tether as far as she could, then stretched out her right front paw even farther, trying to steal the snowball from Wolf. He gave her an I-don't-think-so look and turned away, rolling the ball along with him. Fox sat down and whined. Roy picked up another snowball and tossed it underhand, so it landed at her paws.

Wynter's eyes followed the whole exchange. I swear they softened, seeing Roy's attention to her dogs. "Snowmobiles," she said softly, "are noisy and clunky."

Wait. What? Why would she hit him over the head like that?

Roy turned his back on the dogs. Squaring his shoulders, he stared her down. "Snowmobiles are faster."

"True," Wynter said, "but my dogs can travel as far as a small snowmobile."

Roy's eyes narrowed. "Snowmobiles don't need to be fed."

"But they need gas. Both cost money."

Packrat pulled a white cloth from his pocket and waved it between them. "Truce! You two can't even go two minutes without bickering. Sheesh!"

Wynter smiled at Roy. "That's because—"

Kkkkkrrrrrrk!

Static from my camp radio cut through the almost-fight.

Tugging it from my pocket, I held the button to talk. "Yeah, Mom. What's up?"

"Karl Newman is here for the week." Mom was in business mode. "He registered yesterday and asked for five gallons of water and six bundles of wood to be delivered to his site. He had a few questions for your father, too. But I totally forgot. So, I asked your dad to go over this morning but he's still plowing, and then he has to start packing for the campground owners' conference." Mom sighed. "Could you do it?"

"Karl?" I hadn't expected him. He wasn't seasonal, but he did travel from Vermont every July to rent one of our campers for four weeks.

"You know how he gives his nature conservation talks at libraries and summer camps in the area every year? I suspect—" No sound came from the radio for a few seconds, then, "Sorry, Cooper, it's Molly again. I've got to see what she wants. She's been a little clingy today."

"Just today?" I muttered. But I didn't press the TALK button on the radio when I said it.

"Gotta go, Wynter," Packrat explained. "Time to sign in and get to work."

"No problem," she said. "It's so cool how your mom trusts you to talk to a customer on your own and explain things."

"We'll catch up later?" Packrat asked.

Wynter smiled. "I owe you all a ride."

Packrat, Roy, and I walked back down the camp road, each of us lost in our own thoughts. It was so quiet I could hear the packed snow squelching under our boots.

Wait.

Quiet.

Too quiet.

We all stopped walking. Something was missing.

Summer was missing. I felt like I'd lost my right arm.

The three of us turned to stare at Wynter's campsite. Summer and Wynter were talking a mile a minute as the dogs danced and jumped around them. Only Raven stared at us with a do-you-have-to-go face.

"What the heck?" Roy said. "Didn't she hear you? We have a job to do. Together."

"Oh, she heard." Packrat buried his hands in his pockets and tucked his chin into his sweatshirt, looking as hurt as I was. "What's Wynter got that we don't?" he complained.

I looked him in the eye. "Dogs. Lots and lots of adorable dogs. And a sled."

Still, as we walked down the road in silence, I found myself thinking about two things. One, how easy it was for Summer to ditch us. And two, how much it seemed to bug Packrat that she had.

CHAPTER 6

In the Northeast, lynx mate in March. Their litter is born in May and the kittens are cared for by their mother.

"Geez, she didn't have to dump us cold like that," Packrat grumbled as the three of us reached the end of Wynter's street. I snuck a look at Packrat, while Roy just grunted in response. "I mean, I've kind of gotten used to her hanging around and chirping beside us," he said.

My feet stumbled over nothing at his words. He missed her, too? My thoughts a jumbled mess, I blurted out, "She didn't dump us—she just wants to hang out with Wynter and her dogs."

"Same thing." Packrat shook his head sadly. "Looks like there's competition for Summer this week."

Yeah, but who's competing?

Back when we'd met Summer, right after she'd moved into the house across the lake, I'd thought her pretty cool 'cause she enjoyed wildlife watching in the woods, and from kayaks on the lake almost as much as I did. Packrat liked hanging out with her because she knew a lot about fishing.

Did he *like*-like her now?

Wait. *Did I?*

Half an hour later, my friends and I had loaded the golf cart with Karl's supplies and taken them to his campsite. Parking the cart next to his super-sized pickup truck, which had a blue ATV in the bed, we found a man with salt-and-pepper-colored hair kneeling in the snow, looking under our rental camper.

Parking the golf cart, I leaned on the steering wheel. "Is something wrong?" I asked.

Karl jumped, hitting the top of his head on the sharp, bottom edge of the camper. Sitting back on his heels, he muttered, "Owww!"

The three of us hopped off the cart and rushed over. Seeing him touch his head, I winced along with him.

"Sorry," I apologized. "We didn't mean to startle you."

Standing, hand still on his head, Karl gave us a sheepish look. "I, umm, thought I heard something. Under the camper, that is."

I knelt to take a quick look. Sometimes families of mice moved into an empty camper over the winter. Or raccoons and skunks might seek shelter underneath. But I didn't see any signs of that.

"I don't see anything," I told him.

Packrat bent down to pick up a pile of snow and form it into a flat square. He pulled a washcloth out of a coat pocket, wrapped up the snow, and held it out to Karl. "For your head."

When Karl took his hand off his head to put the snowpack on, I saw a big red mark under his hair. "I'm more embarrassed than anything," he said, "but it already feels better. So, let's start again." Karl put out his free hand for me to shake. "Hey, Cooper! Nice to see you. Your mom said you'd stop by with my supplies. I'm glad I got back before you did."

"Want your wood bundles by the campfire?" I asked, using my best customer-service voice.

"Sure!" Karl sat at the picnic table, still holding the snowpack to his head. "And the water just inside the camper door, please."

"Did you have a presentation today?" I asked, setting a load of wood down and going back for more.

"My first."

"What's your wildlife conservation camp all about?" Packrat handed me a bundle and took one himself.

"I teach about New England animals, our environment, and how we can help them."

Roy frowned and backed away from Karl like he had cooties or something. "You mean you teach school stuff?"

Karl's smile went from ear to ear. "Geez, I hope it isn't school-like! More camp-like." Roy gave an approving look. "I do hands-on activities, like re-creating what it would look like in the snow if an owl and a mouse ran into each other."

The three of us joined him at the picnic table. "Not good for the mouse!" Packrat said.

"Maybe—maybe not!" Karl exclaimed. I swear he wiggled with excitement to have someone to talk to about it. "You'd see an imprint of little mouse tracks through the snow." His middle and pointer fingers walked across the table toward me. "They'd lead to an imprint of spread-out owl's wings, almost like when you flop to the ground to make a snow angel." Both his hands fanned out like angel wings. "And . . . you'd either see the mouse tracks beyond the wings," his fingers walked across the table again, "or you wouldn't. There's so much tracks and prints in the snow can tell us!"

"Cooool." I was the wiggler now. "I wish I could take your class!"

"You can!" Karl put down the snowpack and jumped up from the table. Going up the steps to his camper door, he opened it to reach inside and grab something off his kitchen counter.

Coming back, he held out his brochure to me. I opened it to see pictures of him hiking in the snow with kids. Another picture showed different kids pulling apart owl pellets to find the bones. Still another showed a group of people studying animal tracks in the dirt. I flipped the brochure over eagerly.

Do bears really hibernate?
Learn to identify animal tracks!
Meet my wildlife mascot!

"Earth to Cooper!" Packrat had cupped one hand around his mouth like I was standing across the lake or something.

"You can't go," Roy pointed out. "You've got to run the—"

"Festival!" The three of us shouted it at once. I jumped up from the picnic table. "Great idea!"

Karl's cheeks wiggled as he laughed. This guy was always laughing!

"Wanna fill me in?" he asked.

"We're putting together a winter festival this week! Would you want to run an activity for us?" My arms out, I turned in a circle. "You could take groups of kids into our woods, show them how to track animals." I walked toward the edge of his site and looked to the untouched snow under the trees beyond it. "I bet there's lots our woods could tell you!"

Karl came up beside me, his face serious now. "You know, that sounds perfect. It's exactly what I need!" His smile slowly grew. "Yes! I could make time for a presentation here. I'm at the library Tuesday and Thursday. I think your mom said the fishing derby was Monday, and the main festival day was Saturday?" At my nod, his eyes twinkled. "Let me look at my calendar to find a day that would work for me."

"Hey, speaking of the woods telling us stuff." Packrat waved me over to where he stood near a grouping of three white birch trees. "Check it out. That little lynx gets around!"

I took a few steps closer. "It came through here, too!"

Roy called from the back of the rental trailer. "There's some here, too!"

"Hmm." Karl had gotten serious. He stared at the tracks, and with his thumb and pointer finger, stroked his chin. "Do you have a lot of snowshoe hare around here? If there's lots of hare, there are lynx. In a year when there aren't a lot of hares, they'll move on."

"We saw three lynx just yesterday."

At my words, Karl's eyebrows went up, and I knew he wanted details. But I also saw Packrat and Roy behind him, making time-to-go faces.

"I promised Mom I'd stock our own wood pile for our campfire tonight. You should come," I suggested. "I can tell you more about the lynx we saw. And we'll have hot cocoa."

"With marshmallows." Packrat licked his lips.

"It's not a campfire without them!" Roy scoffed.

"I'll be there," Karl said, but without his typical laughter.

As the three of us walked away, I looked over my shoulder to wave good-bye.

Karl didn't wave back, though. He was staring off into the woods behind his camper, still stroking his chin, deep in thought.

CHAPTER 7

Lynx are related to tigers, lions, and domestic cats.

"What's your favorite kind of campfire?"

Packrat sat on a wooden bench, his hand deep in a package of soft, pink, round marshmallows. Pulling out two, he slid them onto the end of a long, thin wooden roasting stick.

"My favorite?" Using my pointer finger and thumb, I pulled a lightly tanned, gooey, saggy, strawberry marshmallow off my own stick and put it on the square of white chocolate sitting on my graham cracker. Licking my fingers, I put another cracker on top and took a big bite.

"Your favorite campfire," Packrat asked. "Spring, fall, winter, or summer?"

As if on cue, Wynter and Summer walked into the light of the fire. A chair sat empty beside me, and I badly wanted to ask Summer to take it, but the words got stuck in my throat. What if Roy teased me? What if she said no?

Summer plopped into a bench chair with bundled-up Molly, which put her next to Packrat's chair. My chance disappeared. Wynter sat on the other side of Molly.

Roy wore a pained look. "I wouldn't touch that question with a ten-foot fishing pole!"

"C'mon, you guys, do you plan to make fun of our names all week long?" Summer tucked Molly's blanket in around her. "Molly, I've got to warn you." She let my sister snuggle in for warmth. "Boys are weird."

Molly wrinkled her nose. "Cooper's not weird."

Summer tipped her head to one side like she was considering it. "Hmm, I guess you're right. Cooper isn't weird. He can be cool. Sometimes."

The crackle of the campfire suddenly sounded like fireworks in the heavy silence after her words. I think my cheeks were as red as Molly's. I leaned back out of the glow of the campfire to hide my smile.

Packrat put a hand inside a long skinny inside pocket to pull out two more marshmallow sticks, holding one out to Summer and one to Wynter.

Wynter shook her head in a no-thank-you kind of way. "That," she said, pointing to his jacket, "makes you cool, too. It's like a magic coat!"

"He's very cool!" Summer giggled.

Wait. I was cool "sometimes," while Packrat was "very cool"?

Molly clapped her hands together. "Guess! Guess anything! I bet he has it."

Wynter smiled at my sister. "Okay then. Leashes. Dog leashes."

Packrat put a hand inside a waist-high pocket on the outside of his jacket. Holding onto the looped end, he let a blue-and-white leash unfold from his hand.

"But you don't even own a dog!" Summer exclaimed. "Why?"

"Well, duh!" The rude words burst from my lips. "Because sometimes we find dogs roaming around off-leash."

From the corner of my eye, I saw Summer stiffen. I concentrated on sliding another pink marshmallow on my stick and putting it over the fire, while trying to sound more whatever-ish.

"And when we do, we have to parade them around the campground until we find their owner."

"Ahhh," said Wynter.

Mom walked over, brushed some light snow off a chair with her gloved hand, and sat down. Karl walked in from the other side of the fire to do the same. Pulling another droopy marshmallow off my stick, I offered it to Wynter.

"No, thank you." To Molly, Wynter said, "But I'd love a graham cracker. I'm not much of a candy eater. Cookies are my thing. Can't get enough of them."

"Wynter Mint!" Roy blurted.

"Roy?" Mom's did-I-really-just-hear-that voice crossed over the campfire. "Are you making fun of her name?"

"No, Mrs. Wilder. Not really!" Roy scrambled for the right words, fidgeting on the edge of his seat, looking to each of us to help him out so he wouldn't be in hot water with my mom. "I'm trying to figure out her middle name." His explanation came out in a rush. "Wynter's family likes naming in themes, and she said she likes cookies, and mint cookies are the first Christmas cookie that came to mind, and we've got this bet, and—"

Our new friend snorted. "And you thought Wynter Mint was a good guess?" She shoulder-butted a giggling Molly. "Wynter Mint. Wrong. Three guesses left."

Mom opened her mouth to ask more questions.

Time to change the subject.

"Karl, I wondered what your wildlife mascot is?" I asked quickly.

Karl leaned forward and asked, "My mascot?"

"The brochure you showed us. It said you had a mascot."

"What's a mascot?" Molly asked.

Karl leaned back in his chair. "Well, a wildlife mascot is a live animal you bring with you when speaking to the public about wildlife. No matter what the animal is, it represents all nature and how important the animal kingdom is to the balance of our state, and our world. Sometimes, depending on the animal, you can let people hold or pet it. The idea is, if people can experience wildlife up close, they'll appreciate it and take care of it after they leave your talk." He cleared his throat. "Unfortunately, I no longer have mine."

"Did it"—Summer's voice dipped to a whisper—"die?"

"Yes. Yes, it did. I was lucky enough to have an education permit, back home in Vermont, for a little female porcupine." Karl sighed. "Petunia was orphaned under a friend's shed. He'd hand-fed her for a couple of years until he suddenly had to move for his job. So, he contacted me. She couldn't have survived in the wild on her own because she'd imprinted on my friend and relied on him for food. So, I took her in." Karl smiled at the memory. "I suddenly had more presentations on my calendar than I could handle! She was so popular! Most people have their porcupine facts all mixed up, like thinking they can throw their quills, or they carry rabies. Neither of those is true.

"When Petunia presented with me, people left understanding how important porcupines are for our environment. I miss her company, and I miss introducing her to kids at my wildlife conservation talks."

"Which reminds me," Mom said, her eyes meeting mine across the campfire, "what do you have lined up for activities this week? We should write them on the whiteboard in the office and spread the word."

"I'll give dogsled rides," Wynter offered.

"I can take campers on a winter hike to look for signs of wildlife," Karl told her.

A tall, thin woman with short, dark, curly hair stepped into the firelight.

Wynter smiled, "Hey, Mom! You made it!"

"Lisa!" Mom pointed to an empty chair. "Can you sit for a bit?"

"For a minute." Lisa settled in and looked to Wynter. "Did I hear something about giving dogsled rides?"

"Please? It'd be fun! We could take people to the end of the lake and back."

Lisa shook her head. "Wynter, I wish you'd checked with me first. You know we only brought so much food. They'll require much more of it, and many more hours of care if we run them."

"Feel free to charge for the rides," Mom suggested. "No pressure, of course."

"The dogs would like it." Wynter's voice sounded embarrassed. More softly, she added, "I'd like it, Mom."

Lisa crossed her arms. "You aren't doing it alone, I'll tell you that."

Everyone suddenly got fidgety, checking their phones or watches, looking anywhere but at Lisa and Wynter. Packrat jumped up to grab three logs from the woodshed while Roy's knee bounced a mile a minute.

I was embarrassed for Wynter. She had to be a little bit older than us, fifteen or sixteen maybe. We knew plenty of sixteen-year-olds who snowmobiled and snowshoed by themselves. Ice-fished, too. Was Lisa that much of a worrywart?

Or maybe she didn't trust her daughter.

One snowflake fell over the roaring campfire. A second drifted down behind it. Then a third, fourth, and fifth, all at the same time.

All eyes went up toward the darkened sky.

"I'd like a dogsled ride!" Molly's excited words brought our gazes back to her. A snowflake landed on the very tip of her nose. Molly giggled, trying to see it through crossed eyes as it melted there. We all laughed with her. Summer whipped out her phone to take photos.

Lisa didn't laugh, though. She stared at Molly as Summer, then Wynter, took selfies with her. I couldn't read Lisa's expression. Sad? Mad? Confused?

Finally, Lisa said quietly, "I think Wynter and I can make it happen." She nodded to Molly. "You get the first ride."

Molly clapped her mittened hands together. "Yes!"

Headlights hit the camp gate. A pickup truck with the red-and-black Maine Warden Service logo on the driver's door pulled up on the side of the camp road. Warden Kate got out and joined us all at the fire.

Molly threw her head back and yawned so big, I swear we could have fit a moose in her mouth. That had Mom looking at her watch.

"I'm bringing Molly inside," Mom stood. "Take my seat, Kate. I warmed it up for you!"

Warden Kate laughed out loud. It was an old joke, but for some weird reason, all the campers thought it was funny. Especially when the weather got frigid.

Mom walked around the campfire ring to pick up Molly, blanket and all.

"Kate, are you on duty? Would you like me to bring back some coffee?"

"Yes, please. Do you want help?"

"No, no," Mom said as Molly laid her head on her shoulder and closed her eyes. "Is this a social visit or an official one?"

"I had a question for Cooper."

"Oh." The soft comment from Wynter had me sitting a little taller. It wasn't often that Warden Kate came to me with a question. Usually, she came to talk to Mom or Dad. Or she might have a question for a camper who'd witnessed something on the lake.

My marshmallow over the campfire forgotten, I leaned forward in my seat. I felt Packrat, Roy, and Summer do the same.

Mom walked toward the house with Molly as Warden Kate settled in her chair. Finally, she asked me, "Have you four seen any lynx tracks lately?"

Summer, Packrat, Roy, and I took turns telling her what we'd seen, and where.

Warden Kate asked questions, but Wynter didn't jump in; she only followed our conversation with her eyes. We ended by telling Warden Kate about the three lynx we'd seen on the lake yesterday while ice-fishing.

"The children are correct," Lisa assured the warden.

The children are correct?

"Wynter and I were coming across the lake," Lisa explained, "when we saw the two larger lynx back the younger one out onto the ice."

Karl slid forward in his seat. "From what I've learned, they don't mean to do it any harm."

Warden Kate nodded. "I agree. More than likely, they were chasing it off their territory." The warden looked thoughtfully into the flickering flames. "I'm hoping they've all moved on by now."

"Why?" I asked.

She sighed. "I've been investigating claims of a poacher in the area. And this poacher is currently after lynx pelts."

CHAPTER 8

Female lynx will sometimes hunt together, but they won't share their meals.

At Warden Kate's news, my friends and I began talking all at once.

"Lynx pelts!" I jumped up out of my seat. "But—but lynx have been protected from trapping since 1967!"

"Some get trapped accidentally," Summer said hesitantly.

"But they can't be released and have to be reported right away!" Roy insisted.

"Wildlife biologists can trap lynx," Packrat reminded us, "but they do it for research, and they know how to do it safely."

"We've run races up by the border." Wynter looked to her mom. "There have been sightings of lynx with kittens. Their numbers are on the rise, and it's all because of these laws."

I shook my head sadly. "I can't believe some jerk wants to trap them on purpose!"

Lisa waved a hand and gave a quick eye roll.

"You kids need to understand, this sort of thing happens all the time. For every law, there's someone who'll break it. Poachers here in the United States collect furs, then carry them over into Canada. From there, they're shipped to other countries for a big-ticket price." Wynter fidgeted in her seat as her mother kept talking. "Yes, it's wrong. It's illegal. But you can't get so worked up about it. There's nothing you can do. You need to leave it to the authorities." She nodded toward Kate. "And I'm sure they're on top of it."

Warden Kate tipped her head and smiled a small smile to Lisa. To me, she said, "It's why I used the word poacher, and not trapper. A true trapper has taken a ten-hour course. They follow all the rules and understand that these rules were designed for the good of our ecosystem and our wildlife numbers."

"Exactly," Karl said, resting his elbows on his knees. "Poachers are far more interested in the money they can make than they are about ecological balance. Some wouldn't hesitate to take a young one, either."

Each of us became lost in our own thoughts as the campfire crackled and popped, sending sparks up, up, up into the darkness above.

An image of the little lynx we'd seen popped into my mind.

A lynx with a collar.

"Warden?" I hesitated. Had Packrat really seen a collar on it? Maybe it'd been a black mark? *Either way, she'd want to know.* "There's something—"

Pop, pop, pop, pop.

Tires over the snow-covered frozen driveway interrupted me. Another truck, smaller than the warden's, drove through the gate. In the light of its headlights, snowflakes fell lazily. Parking behind Warden Kate, the driver shut the truck off. I noticed it also had a Maine Warden Service logo on the door.

A woman with shoulder-length brown hair stepped out, and Warden Kate stood to wave her over. As the newcomer approached, she greeted us all briefly with a big smile. "This looks cozy!"

Warden Kate pointed to a chair near her. "I'm glad you made it. Everyone, this is Warden Penny. She'll be my assistant in this area for the next few weeks, so I asked her to meet me here. I thought it'd be nice if you got to know her.

"Penny, these are the kids I told you about." With a long look at Wynter's mom, she added, "The ones I work so closely with from time to time." She raised a finger to point us out across the campfire. "Cooper, Packrat, Roy, Summer . . ."

Warden Kate paused, her finger pointing to our newest friend.

"Wynter," I finished for her. "She and her mom are camping here and giving rides Saturday."

"Rides?" Warden Kate asked.

"Dogsledding!" I told her. "And we're putting together a fishing derby. Dad said I needed to talk to you about it first? He would have, but he's leaving for a campground owners' conference."

Warden Kate smiled toward Warden Penny.

"See, I told you. Things are never boring around here. Cooper, tell us about the derby."

The wardens and I were still deep in derby talk when Mom returned carrying a tray with cocoa packets, one giant thermos of coffee, and a second with hot water. There was also a monitor so she could listen for Molly.

As she set the tray down, I realized two things.

One, Packrat and Summer now sat side by side on the bench, shoulder to shoulder, whispering. Summer's face was serious as she talked with her hands. Flicking her hair over her shoulder, she sighed heavily. Packrat looked like he was trying to make her feel better about something. Whatever he said, it made Summer smile a bit.

And two, it bugged me. My stomach felt like it had a rock in it.

I grabbed the poker to jab it in the fire's coals so they wouldn't see me watching them. *Don't show you know*, I told myself.

Summer and Packrat liked each other.

"It'll be mild all week," Mom said.

Somehow, campfire talk always turned to the weather, no matter what season we were in.

"I've been thinking," Mom continued. "The fishing derby is Monday. A bunch of other group activities, like sledding, skating, and snowball target practice are set for next Saturday. What if we plan for Karl's nature walk on Friday morning and have the dogsled rides on Wednesday?"

Wynter, Lisa, and Karl all nodded in agreement.

"That will give me time to scout your trails for potential animal tracks," Karl said.

Pop! Three pea-sized, orange embers jumped from the fire ring, landing by his boot. He kept talking as he smudged them into the ground to be sure they were good and out.

"Cooper told me it'd be okay to snowshoe off your trails?" he asked.

"Absolutely!" Mom assured him. "We have several hiking trails stretching from the back of our property to the shoreline. Cooper can show you on the map."

"Besides the festival, what else are you looking forward to, for vacation week?" Warden Kate asked, blowing across her coffee.

"Snowshoeing," Summer said.

"Getting over to Piehl Mountain," I said.

A military plane had crashed there about fifty years ago and there was a memorial site on the mountain; I wanted to show it to my friends.

"Building a fort and camping out," Packrat chimed in.

"Snowmobiling." Roy shot a challenging glance at Wynter.

She gazed back at him calmly and said, "Skijoring."

Packrat whipped around. "Skijoring?"

"Skijoring," Wynter explained, "is when you wear cross-country skis, but you're pulled by a dog."

Summer's face lit up. "Oooo! I want to try! Can you show us? Does Fox know how to—"

Raaaaaaaarrrrrrrr! Raaaaaaaarrr!

The sound split the night. Everyone leaned forward where we sat, except Karl, who jumped up to spin toward the noise behind him in the woods. He didn't even notice his hot cocoa slosh out of his mug onto his boots.

The whole forest went silent. We waited, listening.

Raaaaaaaarrrrrrr! Raaaar!

Warden Kate took a sip of coffee, gazing at me thoughtfully over the rim and raising her right eyebrow.

Warden Penny started to say something, but Warden Kate put a hand on her arm and gave a quick shake of her head as if to say *Wait a minute.*

"It's the lynx," I said. "Maybe one of the ones we saw earlier?"

"Whoa!" Summer breathed.

Raaaaaaaaaar!

"Possibly, yes," Warden Kate confirmed.

Karl sat back down. We all waited, listening. After a minute or two, I heard rustling as everyone relaxed a bit, shifting in their seats.

Lisa broke the silence. "I've heard them call like this twice before."

"You have?" Wynter exclaimed. "You never told me!"

"It's an early memory, from my days as a teen, camping out in the barn with our dogs. I didn't get a wink of sleep the rest of the night after hearing it! I've never forgotten, so eerie and wild." She paused. "The other time, happened right before you..."

Lisa's voice trailed off. Her face reminded me of the way people look when they walk into a room and hear everyone talking about them.

Wynter became suddenly fixated on digging into the snow with the toe of her boot. Neither one seemed as if they'd finish the memory for us. There was a story there, but I didn't think it had to do with the lynx call.

Karl stared beyond the fire, into the dark of the woods. "Yes, very wild."

"I'll never forget that call!" Roy shook his head. "And I thought fox calls could be creepy."

"What do you think it's calling for?" Karl asked. "Is it hungry? Lost? Lonely?"

Warden Kate shrugged. "Not much is known about lynx vocalizations, but this one isn't very far away. I suspect it's calling to connect with another lynx."

"They are so stealthy, blending in well with their surroundings," Penny explained. "You wouldn't even know they were nearby. What a treat to hear their call." She drank the last of her coffee, set the mug on the tray, and looked to Mom. "Thank you for the pick-me-up before my shift."

Packrat grabbed the marshmallow bag, white chocolate bars, and graham crackers, stuffing them back into his pockets. Warden Kate and Penny picked up their gloves and stood.

"Warden?" I interrupted, before they could leave. "The little lynx we were telling you about? There's something you need to hear. Something Packrat saw."

Warden Kate turned toward him.

"It has a collar," Packrat began. He went on to explain exactly what he'd seen.

Warden Kate shook her head sadly. "I'd say the little lynx is an abandoned exotic animal."

Exotic? I must have misheard. "But lynx are native to Maine."

Warden Penny slapped her gloves on her thigh, once, twice. "What it means is someone dropped their pet off on your property because they didn't want it anymore."

"That's so sad," Wynter said.

"Sad? It's mean!" I threw my hands in the air. "What if it doesn't know how to catch food? I'd like to take that owner and drop them in the middle of the northern Maine woods with no food. See how they'd like it!"

Karl cleared his throat. "You're right, Cooper. If someone adopts exotic wildlife, then they need to be prepared to follow through and care for their pet for as long as they live. Like I did with Petunia."

"Owning a lynx in Maine is illegal, though," Packrat reminded us, "which puts it on a whole other level. I bet there's a big fine for abandoning an animal like that."

Wardens Penny and Kate nodded.

Suddenly, I realized two things.

One, if Warden Kate and Penny were right, then the lynx might be so used to people, it would approach anyone who had food.

And two, the little lynx kitten would be easy prey for that poacher.

CHAPTER 9

Lynx can jump twelve to thirteen feet from a sitting position.

"Is it big enough?" Packrat, Roy, and I stood inside a twelve-by-twelve-foot square drawn in the snow.

"Looks about right," Packrat offered.

"We can always go bigger if we have to," Roy agreed.

The three of us clipped snowshoes to our boots and stomped around, packing down the snow. I'd convinced Mom to let us build a snow fort on one of the biggest, flattest campsites we had, in an empty section of the campground. Packrat, Roy, and I planned to make it our base camp for the week.

Ever since the wardens suggested the little lynx was an abandoned pet, I'd schemed with Packrat and Roy, trying to find a way to check on the lynx kitten. I had to know if it was surviving on its own. And since we only heard it at night, we needed to sneak out after dark to do it. A full moon

and clear sky the next couple of nights would help, and so would sleeping out in a snow fort that was not under the watchful eye of my mother.

Packrat, Roy, and I had spent hours researching winter camping. Our first idea had been to hollow out a mountain of snow, like when we were little kids digging tunnels into the ten-foot-high piles Dad had made with the tractor. That kind of fort had come with a bunch of DANGER and CAVE-IN warnings, though, so we decided we should go with Plan B.

Setting up a tent on the flattened snow, we then created three-foot-high snowball walls all the way around it, leaving room for a door. From what we'd read, the walls would break the wind and help keep our body heat inside the tent. After putting our camp cots inside the fort, we then dug out a fire ring, and rolled snowballs to put around it as chairs.

When we were done, I stood back to proudly look over our campsite.

"I feel like we're forgetting something," Packrat mused.

Roy bent down to pick up some snow. Rolling it into a ball, he then passed it from hand to hand, looking thoughtful. "Tent, fire ring for cooking, camp chairs. Hmm." He drew his arm back, ready to lob the snowball over our snow fort into the road.

All of a sudden, a brown blur plowed through the snow from the woods on our left, exploding through one of our snowball chairs before launching itself at Roy's arm. Missing, the blur body-slammed our friend, sending the two of them to the ground, wildly rolling around.

"Wyyyyyyynter!" Roy hollered.

Arooooooooo! howled Moose.

Packrat and I doubled over laughing. I swear that dog could sense a ball being thrown from a mile away! I laughed so hard I could barely speak, while Roy wiggled around on the ground, trying to keep the snowball from Moose.

Wynter rushed into the campsite from her dog's trail, her worried eyes searching everywhere. Seeing Moose and Roy, she stopped and relaxed. "Oh, thank goodness! I thought Moose had caught a skunk." With a twinkle in her eye, she added, "Well, actually . . ."

Packrat had to sit down to catch his breath from laughing so hard. "Good one, Wynter!"

Roy's arm shot out of the coat and fur pile, launching the snowball toward the woods. Moose took off after it like a rocket! Roy lay on his back, arms and legs spread out, staring up at the bright blue sky. Wynter stood above him, looking down, hands on her hips. "You hurt or something?"

Roy scowled up at her.

"Just his pride," I said.

Moose trotted back to lick Roy from his chin to his forehead. Sitting up, my friend wiped his face with his coat sleeve. "Dog slobber!" he grumbled. I could tell from the way his scowl wavered that he wasn't as mad as he wanted to be. Until he looked up at Wynter again, and then the full scowl reappeared. "Can't you train that dog or something?"

Wynter gave my arm a light shove, and asked, "Can't you train your friend or something?"

Her laughter sounded like tinkling bells. Her smile, bright. I couldn't help it; I laughed out loud right along with her.

Packrat coughed once. Twice. Three times. "Umm, Coop? Cooper!"

"Ahem!" Summer stood on the edge of the campsite, Raven at her side. "I looked up from rolling my snowball and you were gone!"

The words were obviously for Wynter, but Summer's left boot tapped the snow and her eyes flashed in annoyance toward both of us. What the heck? What'd I do?

"You making a snowman or something?" Roy said, giving me an isn't-that-cute wink as he stood to brush off his pants.

Summer shifted all her annoyance directly toward him.

"So? What if I am? We finished our fort a long time ago. We were waiting for you!"

I looked between Packrat and Roy. Finished? We didn't even know they'd started!

Summer whipped around, her ponytail flapping in annoyance. The rest of us followed behind like little ducklings after an angry mother duck. Even Raven and Moose fell into line.

Following the trail in the snow and stepping around trees and shrubs, Summer led us through a thirty-foot patch of woods to the edge of the next cleared area with a fire ring.

"Your mom gave us our own campsite." Summer stuck out a mittened hand toward their fort in a ta-da kind of way.

My jaw dropped open. Their snow fort had five-foot-high walls in the shape of a square, in the back corner of the site so the trees and brush protected two sides of it. The front of the fort stood higher than the back. Across the top, like a roof, they'd staked a tarp and over that had laid pine boughs.

Wynter walked to the doorway and pushed a tarp-door to one side. "Go inside. Check it out." She tipped her head toward the opening. "You know you want to."

Roy laughed in a this-oughta-be-good kind of way. I followed, ducking through the doorway head down, then raising my eyes as I stepped inside.

I could stand up at this end! And they'd built snow beds into the back wall!

"But," Packrat asked Wynter as he sat on one, "won't you get cold sleeping on snow?"

"We'll put an air mattress between the snow and us," Wynter explained.

"I bet we'll be warmer in our fort tonight than you are in this one!" The minute the words were out of Roy's mouth, I could tell by the way his eyes darted between Packrat and mine, he regretted them. I mean, wasn't one bet with Wynter enough?

Summer clapped her hands together. "Ha! I knew Roy couldn't resist betting on our forts! How can we tell who stays warmer?"

"Thermometers," Roy and Wynter said at the same time.

Hearing boots crunching outside, Wynter slid the door flap aside and we all stepped out to find Dad and Warden Penny walking down the road.

The warden raised her hand in greeting. "This is quite a clever setup! And so is the one next door. Are you all spending the night?"

"Umm, yes?" I looked at Dad hopefully. I hadn't gotten so far as to ask him or Mom about sleeping out overnight yet.

Dad shrugged. "I'm okay with it. Of course, you know your mom will go over the winter camping do's and don'ts checklist first."

She'll go over it a gazillion times, I thought. *But it'll be worth it.*

"Temperatures tonight will be in the upper twenties. With proper clothing, they'll be fine. No inside heaters, though," the warden cautioned. "And keep a flap open a little bit so the fresh air can seep in. I'd be happy to talk to your mom and put in a good word."

"Yes, please!" I knew her approval would go a long way toward getting Mom to agree to it.

"The warden lost a glove last night," Dad said. "Since you three put out the campfire," he looked to Packrat, Roy, and me, "we wondered if you might have found it?"

I looked at my friends; we shook our heads.

"If I had a nickel for every glove I've lost," Warden Penny chuckled. "Well, have fun with your fort this week! Don't eat too many s'mores!" she teased.

She and Dad started to walk away, but then the warden turned back.

"Oh, Cooper, I almost forgot. Kate wanted me to follow up on those lynx kitten tracks. Exactly where did you see them?"

"There were some at my campsite," Wynter offered. "Number twenty."

"Karl's site had them, too," I told the warden. "Site thirty-three. There's nothing but woods behind both, and the lake beyond that. Do you want us to take you there?"

"No, I'll get a map from your mom on the way out. I'll ask around the area," Warden Penny said, "and see if anyone knows if someone came through with a lynx as a pet. Maybe I can track down the owner and figure out who abandoned it, and why. Let me know if you see the kitten or its tracks again?"

We all nodded.

As Warden Penny and Dad left, Packrat said to me, "Maybe we'll have something to report to the warden after—"

Roy shoved Packrat's shoulder with his own and gave him a don't-you-dare-tell look.

Packrat rubbed his shoulder, shooting back a what-the-heck look.

I was just as confused. Roy didn't want us to tell the girls we were tracking the lynx tonight. Why?

"After what?" Summer asked suspiciously.

"After supper," Roy fibbed.

Wynter's eyes glanced between us all. I had to smooth things over and fast!

"Supper on our site," I said. "We're gonna listen for the lynx again. Want to join us?"

Summer's eyes grew steely. Her left cheek twitched.

I held my breath.

"Fine," she said. Leaning in, she whispered to me, "I know you're all up to something."

She wasn't wrong. I just wished she could be in on it with us.

CHAPTER 10

Lynx kittens stay with their mother for a full year.

After leaving Summer and Wynter's campsite, Packrat, Roy, and I
cleaned the bathrooms in the office and helped Mom close up for the
night by sweeping and washing the store floor.

"Promise me you'll be careful out there." Mom held up her walkie-
talkie-like radio and waggled it as we bundled up to leave. "Mine will
be on, and next to my bed. You keep yours on, too. If any of you gets
too cold, the door to the house will be open, okay? I've put a stack of
blankets in the living room, and extra pillows, and——"

"Mom!" I cut her short, or I knew we'd be here all night. "We get
it, really!"

She laughed and leaned over to kiss me. I rolled my eyes while
offering my cheek and stepped back afterward. Roy gave a half-cough,
half-laugh behind me, and from the corner of my eye, I saw Packrat
elbow him in the ribs in a knock-it-off way.

Mom ruffled Roy's short red hair and chuckled. "Okay, okay. I'll let
you guys go. Remember, the door's always open."

I lingered behind, letting Roy and Packrat go before me.

"Thanks, Mom." I shot her a smile over my shoulder before closing
the door.

It was only five o'clock at night. If this was a summer day, the sun
would still be hours from setting, and the campground would be ringing

with the sounds of kids playing, people laughing, bikes zipping past, everyone having fun. My friends and I probably would have been fishing in the middle of the lake, or swimming to cool off after raking campsites or splitting wood.

Now, in the dead of winter, the sun had already dipped below the tree line, making a soft orange glow behind it. The bare trees around our site stood black against a light blue sky. And everything was so very still. I swear I'd have heard a mouse if it had scurried by, but I would have warned against it. The full February Snow Moon had risen to shine through the bare trees and reflect off the snow. When it rose higher in the sky later, it'd light up the forest like a giant spotlight. Just what we needed for stalking lynx.

On our very own snowy campsite, bundled up in hats, scarves, gloves, coats, and boots, we started a campfire and sat around, waiting for the girls to arrive. I got as close to the roaring campfire as I could without melting my snowball chairs or burning off my eyebrows. The light of the flames only reached as far as our circle of chairs. Hot dogs sizzled on the grate. They smelled amazing! My stomach growled as Packrat rolled them over and flipped the rolls too.

"You should listen to them tell the story, Wynter! Cooper and Packrat set up a fake tent to fool their parents so they could stake out an eagle nest overnight. There were even fake snoring sounds!"

I smiled as I heard Summer chattering to Wynter as they headed our way. Sound travels a lot farther in colder weather, and we heard her words clearly.

"See?" Wynter's voice teased. "This is how I know you like-like him! You're always talking about him, and telling me stories."

"Is it that obvious?" Summer's voice grew quieter, even though they were closer.

Packrat was the one who made the fake snoring sounds happen, I thought sadly. *I was right. She likes him!*

"Summer," Roy muttered under his breath, making me miss Wynter's answer to her. He jammed his poking stick under the grate and into the red coals over and over again. "I bet she talks in her sleep!" Lifting out the stick, he watched the red and yellow flame eat up the end of it for a couple of seconds before sticking it back in the fire.

"Was Roy there, too?" Wynter's voice was even closer now.

"Yep. Those three are always together," Summer replied as the girls stepped onto our site.

Packrat jumped up. "Need a seat?" he asked Summer, even though the chair on the other side of him was empty.

She sat down beside him, not looking at me. Packrat pulled tongs out of his coat pocket. Taking a roll, he plopped a hot dog inside, holding out the first one to Summer with a wide smile. "There's ketchup and mustard on the table. Relish, too." He looked toward our picnic table. "Want me to get them?"

"I'm a little hungry, too, you know!" Roy barked.

"I'll get it," I quickly said. I needed to do something because all of a sudden, I didn't know what to say to Summer.

Packrat offered the next hot dog to Wynter.

"I can wait," she said, waving a hand toward Roy. "Give it to him. He looks like he's about to faint from hunger."

I sat back down and handed Summer the ketchup.

"Thanks." She paused. "How'd you know I liked ketchup?"

I shrugged. I knew she liked ketchup on hot dogs, mayo on hamburgers, and mustard on her ham sandwiches. But I wasn't about to tell her that.

"It's not too cold tonight," she said. "Ready to test our forts?"

Packrat finished handing out the hot dogs, took one for himself, and sat down on the other side of Summer. "Our thermometer is in our fort already. Get ready to lose!"

"We've been researching," I warned jokingly.

"Yeah, we figured out the right clothing and bedding and stuff like that," Roy told the girls between bites of hot dog.

"Well, I've got the bunkmate with more wilderness camping experience than all of us put together!" Summer put her arm around Wynter. "*You* guys better get ready to lose!"

The banter went back and forth. It felt good to laugh over a campfire again, just me and my friends.

An hour later, the woods were pitch black around us and bright stars twinkled above. The grate lay beside the fire ring, and with five large logs added to the embers, it blazed hot and high. Feeling the cold seeping into my boots, I wiggled my toes in their wool socks and stretched my legs so my feet were closer to the fire. Grabbing my mini flashlight off the table beside me, I shined it on my watch.

"Why do you care what time it is?" Summer asked softly. "You've got nowhere to go tonight, do you?"

"So, what do we know about lynx?" Packrat asked before I had to answer her. He pulled his tablet out from an inside pocket of his jacket.

"Seventy-five percent of their diet is snowshoe hares," Wynter offered. "Any of those around here?"

"Yes," I said, grateful to have something else to talk about.

"Their young are called kittens." Summer sighed. "Wish I could see a litter of them. Remember when we found the fox kits?"

"I do!" I grinned, remembering how the two of us had found five fox kits one day, staying long enough to watch them cautiously come out of their spring den one by one to study us.

But Summer leaned over Packrat's arm now, as he typed words into the search bar. Scanning the results, he told us, "It says lynx are endangered and it's illegal to hunt them anytime."

"We knew that," Wynter said.

"And it says a full-grown lynx is thirty-two to forty inches, head to butt."

Roy frowned. "The one we saw seemed smaller."

"Agreed," I said, getting up to look over Packrat's shoulder. "I bet ours is under a year old."

"Now what do we know about poaching?" Packrat's face was lit up from the glow of his screen. He clicked on a website about game wardens and their jobs.

"Well, lots of people think it's only a problem in Asia or Africa with animals like tigers and elephants," I said. "But it happens right here in the United States, too!"

"Bears are poached for their hides and their paws," Wynter told us.

"I read an article which said a hundred million sharks die every year when poachers take their fins, then leave them to die in the water," Roy said sadly.

"But why?" Summer's eyes glistened in the firelight.

"Well, the horns of a bighorn sheep can sell for twenty thousand dollars on the black market. Shark fins are probably worth a lot, too."

"It's all about getting rich." Packrat spat out the words as he looked at his screen.

Roy leaned in on Packrat's right.

"Wait! Am I reading that right? Two hundred and seventy-five dollars?" Roy exclaimed. "For one lynx fur?"

"What?" Summer leaned over Packrat's arm to look. "Three hundred and sixty!" she breathed, pointing farther down the screen.

Roy raised an eyebrow as Packrat scrolled down some more.

The four of us gasped. "Fifteen hundred dollars?"

"That can't be right!" Wynter cried.

Jumping up, she came to see for herself. "Click on the link there. The *About Us* tab." As she scanned the page, her shoulders relaxed. "See?" she said. "These sellers say they only deal with hides and fur ethically. Which means the fur was obtained by *legal* means. There are a few places in Canada where you can hunt them, you know." She pointed to the screen. "The last line says they won't take in lynx furs which have been illegally hunted."

"*Pffft!*" Roy's voice went up a notch. "And you believe everything you read?"

"You don't?" Wynter's voice met his and her eyes narrowed. "There are good trappers, you know!"

"We do know," I assured her. "We have friends who hunt and trap. *Legally*. What we're dealing with here is illegal."

Roy leaned toward Wynter. "You seem to know a little something about trapping." It wasn't a question.

"It's a family thing."

If it'd been summertime, we'd have heard chirping crickets. Instead, I swear we heard frost forming.

Wynter took a step back from us. "I'm a little cold. Ready for bed?" she asked Summer.

Summer's eyes locked on mine. I knew she still wondered what we were planning, and she wanted in on it. Still, she nodded to Wynter.

Packrat reached into a small outer coat pocket to pull out an outdoor thermometer. He held it out to Wynter and asked, "What's the winner get?"

"The loser has to make the winner pancakes over the fire for breakfast," she suggested.

Summer smiled. "We'll take ours with blueberries."

Packrat pulled the thermometer out of reach.

"What?" Summer teased, tugging the thermometer from his hand. "Worried?"

Wynter laughed. "Too late, the bet's been sealed!"

"Just put it in the middle of your fort!" Roy said gruffly. "No cheating by tucking it into your sleeping bag."

The moon hung high now, lighting up the woods around us. The shadows cast around us were long. The girls walked back to their fort by way of the road, not even needing a flashlight.

Who-cooks-for-you? Who-cooks-for-you-all?

The barred owl's call slipped through the winter night, as it tried to connect with its mate. Nesting season would start soon.

An answering call came from farther away.

Who-cooks-for-you? Who-cooks-for-you-all?

"So," I asked Roy, "why didn't you let me ask Summer along on our hunt for the lynx tonight?"

"I think we have to consider Wynter a suspect," he said. "And right now, where Wynter goes, Summer goes."

"Wynter's a suspect?" Packrat asked.

"Her mom could be the poacher Warden Kate is looking for," Roy said. "They're from Canada. Wynter knows something about lynx and other wildlife. She's really defensive about trapping. Besides, if she's a dogsledder, she and her mom can travel long distances in one day," Roy said.

Darn. He had a couple of good points there.

I stared into the fire. Wynter? I hadn't known her long, but I couldn't picture her taking animals illegally. Especially an endangered one like a lynx.

Wynter after a lynx pelt? Nah.

But I'd been fooled before.

CHAPTER 11

*Lynx live up to fifteen years in the wild and
approximately twenty-six years in captivity.*

Packrat, Roy, and I were still talking an hour later by the roaring
campfire, when I heard *Kkkkkrrrrrrk!*

My camp radio. It could only be one person at nine o'clock at night.

"Cooper?"

"Yeah, Mom?"

Roy and Packrat shared a look. Roy waggled his eyebrows and
mouthed the next words perfectly in time with Mom.

"Are you warm enough?"

"Yes." I looked skyward, shaking my head.

Packrat snorted. Then he mouthed back, "Remember, the door is open."

"The door is open if you get too cold."

We all chuckled—my finger off the button, of course.

"Oh, and Cooper?"

"Yeah, Mom?"

"Tell Packrat and Roy to stop making fun of me."

We burst out laughing. This time, I kept the button held down so
Mom could hear it.

"Sorry, Mrs. Wilder," they both called into the radio.

"Just stay warm!" Mom's voice held a hint of a smile. "I don't want
to be defrosting three boy-sized ice cubes tomorrow."

I dropped the radio into my coat pocket, then checked my watch
again. Five after nine.

I took off my gloves and tucked them under my left armpit before standing to put my bare hands over the hot flames. We heard the girls murmuring at the campsite next door through the stillness of the cold night, but I couldn't make out the words. Were they scheming to find the lynx on their own? Summer wouldn't hesitate to do it, and Wynter was a nature geek like me. Between the two of them, they'd have good ideas.

Or were they talking about us? What would Summer say to Wynter about me?

I shook my head. What the heck? Why did I care? After watching Summer and Packrat tease each other over the thermometer, I just knew they liked each other.

I checked my watch again and sat back down on my snow chair. Not even nine-fifteen. Forty-five minutes to go.

Raaaaaaaarrrrrrrr! Raaaaaaarrr!

Packrat, Roy, and I jumped to our feet, our travel-sized Monopoly board flipping off the snowball chair and sending pieces all over the ground.

"The lynx!" Packrat breathed.

"It's so close!" Roy zipped up his coat.

We'd heard this call before! At the campfire with Warden Kate! "The connection call," I reminded my friends. Maybe we'll see two lynx! "Time to track it." Packrat pulled a flashlight out of his pocket.

"But not with that!" Roy cautioned, pointing at Packrat's flashlight. "It'll make us night-blind."

Packrat pushed a button on the end of his flashlight. A white beam hit the Monopoly mess on the ground. He pushed the button again, and the beam turned red.

I raised an eyebrow at Roy. Of course Packrat had an infrared flashlight!

"We won't need it yet, though," I said. "The moon will light our way."

We quickly picked up the game board and pieces as we waited for the next call.

Raaarrrr!

Softer now, but still nearby.

The three of us made eye contact. I pointed at the woods across the road from our campsite.

Raaaarrrr! Hissssss!

In the summer we could wear sneakers on leaf-littered campground trails and be fairly quiet. But here in the winter woods, our big boots clomped, and there were spots of thin ice under the snow which cracked when we unwittingly stepped on them. So, we traveled carefully, listening, watching, and trying to judge exactly where the lynx was.

With each call, we changed our direction slightly.

Raaarrrrr!

Rrrrraaaaaarrrr!

I put out my hand to signal my friends to hold up for a second. The lynx calls sounded slightly different. I held up two gloved fingers toward Packrat and Roy and raised my eyebrows. Roy shrugged, but Packrat nodded. He'd heard it, too. Was one of the adults bullying the little one again?

The snow glowed bright white under the full moon, while the shadows of the woods seemed blacker. I imagined all kinds of nocturnal animals hiding in those dark, shadowy places, watching us as we snuck through the woods.

Knowing we were close to the lynx, we traveled from tree to tree now, scanning the woods for any signs of them: tracks, fleeing rodents, broken branches, or tufts of fur on shrubs. Packrat didn't dare leave his flashlight on, but every now and then he'd shoot the red beam at something to check it out.

Suddenly, the woods rang loudly with a lynx's call. It sounded different from the connection call, though. Kind of panicky.

"It's in trouble!" I whispered urgently.

The second lynx replied to the first. What the heck was happening out there?

We jogged now between trees and bushes, pushing aside branches along the way. Any sounds we made were covered up by lynx calls.

Seeing a group of young birch saplings, I signaled Packrat and Roy to head for them. The lynx calls sounded like they were coming from just beyond it, and we could use the trees as cover to check out what the heck was happening.

Slowly we pushed through the branches when—*oooph!* I ran smack into a soft, tall wall!

Packrat ran into my back and Roy into him.

"Owww!" Roy rubbed his forehead. "You have a hard head, Packrat!"

"Yours isn't exactly made of feathers!" Packrat whispered, turning on his flashlight to see what we'd run into.

A white tent-like blind stood before us, with birch tree trunk designs all over it.

"What the heck?" I whispered.

We walked around to the front and unzipped the door. I poked my head inside to find a single three-legged stool in front of the window screen. Someone had sat here, watching what passed through the woods.

My woods!

"Any idea who—" Roy began.

"No!"

We heard the lynx cry out again, and this time it was mixed with a rattling sound, like metal on metal.

Packrat sucked in a breath and pointed off to our right.

There, in the moonlight, walking across the snow, was a lynx. Not the lynx kitten, though. This was one of the full-grown ones. It padded on top of the snow, pacing back and forth.

Raaaaaaar!

Going up on its hind legs, looking just like a cat about to jump up on a counter, it pushed at something dark and box-like with its front paws before dropping back to all fours and pacing again.

"Packrat," I whispered. "I hate to do it, but you have to shine your red light over there."

"Does it have something cornered?" Roy wondered aloud.

When the light hit the box, the adult lynx crouched to stare our way.

I gasped. Not at the lynx, but the box. It was a trap! A man-made log trap. Two eyes glowed from the inside.

Raaaaaaaaaar! Hissssss!

Another lynx—the lynx kitten!

The bigger lynx backed off about ten feet. Packrat shut off his light.

"Maybe it's trying to save the kitten inside!" I cried. "C'mon! We've got to help it!"

I pushed aside some branches and charged forward to lead the way.

I'd only taken a single step when something grabbed the back of my coat and jerked me backwards into the birches again.

CHAPTER 12

Lynx are excellent night hunters. They can spot prey in the dark from 250 feet away.

"No way!" hissed a familiar voice. "I'm taking you back to camp now. Our mothers will never forgive me if I let you——"

"Wynter!" Summer's voice cut her off. "Cooper knows what he's doing. Let him go save the kitten!"

Wynter huffed. But she let go of my collar.

Summer having my back like that made me stand a little taller.

"What are you two doing here anyway?" Roy's question was for both of them, but he stared hard at Wynter.

"Same thing you are!" Wynter leaned forward until she came almost nose to nose with him. "We heard the lynx. We came."

"We thought it'd run into trouble," Summer insisted. She shifted her eyes to me, and they narrowed a bit. "I knew you'd be out here."

Raaaaaaar!

"We don't have time for this!" I turned away from my bickering friends and Summer's angry look.

Parting the branches, I stepped out into the open again. From what I'd read about lynx, I knew they were shy and shouldn't attack. Any other regular night, I'd be happy staying hidden, watching and learning about them. But I didn't have a choice. No way was I letting a poacher take this little pet kitten!

"I'm going in," I said firmly. "The rest of you wait here."

Packrat stepped up next to me. "As if. I'm coming, too."

It was no surprise when Roy moved to stand on my other side.

I heard Summer take a step forward, but Wynter whispered something, and she stopped. I didn't have time to wonder why Summer chose Wynter over saving the lynx. But I did have time to realize it bugged me.

Walking slowly toward the trap, I kept one eye on the adult lynx. It hissed again, softly, but it backed away some more.

"We want to help," I whispered soothingly. I knew it didn't understand my words, but I hoped it would sense what we were trying to do.

It backed away again, not taking its eyes off us. We took a few more steps, and then it turned and sprinted for a nearby shadow.

Reaching the two-by-two-foot log box, I noticed it had a mesh-type wire across the top and bottom. The door was shut, and it was dark inside, but I could make out an outline of the lynx kitten.

"It's okay," I whispered to it. At my voice, it leaned against the back wall, which made the trap wobble. Roy held it firm.

Crouching down so I wouldn't tower over the lynx, I looked inside the trap until I found the release mechanism. All I had to do now was push on it to open the door.

"I need a stick!" I said.

Packrat opened his coat to pull out one of his long skinny marshmallow sticks. Slowly, so as not to panic the lynx, I poked it down into the cage. To my surprise, the lynx stayed calm.

"Should I shine the light in there?" Packrat whispered.

At his voice, the lynx shifted again. The adult lynx called from the shadows nearby.

I poked around the floor of the trap. "C'mon—c'mon!"

Again, a hand grabbed a fistful of my coat and tugged. "We've got to go now!" Wynter's panicked voice filled my ear.

"Not until I free the lynx!" I shrugged her off.

"Cooper?" Summer's voice, urgent and scared. "Two flashlights coming this way."

Standing, I scanned the woods. Two beams of light approached, one from our left, the other from our right.

I looked down at the lynx through the top of the cage. It pressed itself up against the side wall, staring back with wide eyes. Seeing its collar reminded me that it had had a life in a home, being cared for and protected. How did it get here? It must be so scared!

"Quick! Help me pick up the trap!" I cried. "I can't leave it here!"

"No time!" Wynter pleaded with me. "It's made of logs. It's huge! Heavy! It'll take three of us to carry it and will slow us down." When I didn't budge, she hissed, "My mom used to tell me horrible stories about poachers and the things they'll do to protect their stuff! What if they come after us?"

"She's right, Cooper," Packrat urged. "We've seen their trap. That's bad enough. But now we'll see them too, if we stay."

"I'm with Cooper," Roy said. "We stay and fight."

"There's no telling what people like that would do to a bunch of kids!" Wynter cried. "We've got to go now!"

"Cooper?" Summer asked softly. I knew she'd do whatever I asked. I wanted to stay and free the lynx. But putting my friends in danger?

"I can't risk any of you getting hurt," I said to Roy. "Let's go call Warden Kate."

My friends reluctantly turned to go. I gave the lynx one last look.

"I'm sorry," I whispered. "I'm getting help—I'll be back!"

Turning, I followed my friends as fast as I could.

But it felt wrong. So, so wrong.

CHAPTER 13

Newborn lynx kittens can weigh between six and fourteen ounces. Adult lynx weigh between eleven and thirty-seven pounds.

When we were far enough away from whoever was coming through my woods, I pulled out my camp radio.

"Mom!" I half-talked, half-whispered. "Mom! You there?"

We couldn't run through the snow, but we fast-walked, making me sweat under my winter coat.

"Cooper?" Her sleepy voice became more alert by the second. "What's wrong?"

"Call Warden Kate! There's a lynx in a trap between our campsite and the lake."

"On our land? Wait, what are you doing in the woods at midnight? Oh, never mind. We'll talk about that later. Head for the store; I have her home number in my office. Be careful!"

An hour later, the five of us stood looking out the store window. We were waiting for the warden, and the policeman she'd called for backup, to return from their trek in the woods to find the lynx and the trap. I couldn't stop pacing. I kept picturing the kitten's scared eyes as we'd left it behind to face the poachers. Was it okay? Were the people with the flashlights working together? Did one of them take the lynx?

Or worse?

I shuddered.

"I see lights!" Summer exclaimed, her nose leaving prints on the window from trying so hard to see beyond our store's porch lights into the dark beyond. "Three lights!"

"Three flashlights?" Mom mused. "But Kate and the policeman went in alone."

As the figures stepped from the shadowy woods into the light, I saw the third flashlight holder was Warden Penny. The policeman held the arm of a short, stocky man, his head hung down, his hands behind his back. Wardens Kate and Penny each held a side of the trap.

I backed out of the pile of people and turned toward the door.

"Whoa!" Mom put a hand on my arm. "Where do you think you're going?"

"I have to know what happened!"

I opened the store door and ran full force into Wynter's mom, knocking her back a couple of feet. Lisa muttered some angry words under her breath which I didn't quite hear. I knew it wasn't because I'd just plowed into her. I backed up, and she came in, slamming the door shut behind her. Looking past me as if I weren't even there, Lisa lifted her chin toward my mom. "You need to control your son!"

Whoa. Wait—what?

Wynter grabbed her mom's coat at the elbow. "Moooooom! Stop! You're embarrassing me!"

"Embarrassed? That's what you're worried about?" Lisa shook her off. To my mom she said, "From what I've witnessed in my short time here, you allow your son to *play* at being a game warden, letting him get into all kinds of mischief, constantly interfering in Warden Kate's duties."

"Mom!" Wynter whispered, her eyes panicked. "He's not . . ."

My mother slowly and carefully put the Wilder Family Campground coffee mug she'd been holding onto a shelf next to some canned carrots. Facing Lisa, her eyes glinted in anger. Her cheekbone twitched. "Excuse me?"

Lisa had just poked my mama bear.

"You walk into my campground office and proceed to tell me how to raise my son?" Mom's voice became low and dangerous. This was the voice I never argued with. "Our house rules are our business, and I'm not discussing them with you."

"Way to go, Mrs. Wilder," Roy whispered under his breath.

"Listen." Mom's eyes softened a touch. "I get it. You're upset that Wynter was out there in a potentially dangerous situation, but Cooper didn't drag her out there, and he didn't keep her there."

"It's true!" Wynter stepped between her mom and mine. "I went out on my own, Mom. I dragged Summer with me."

Summer frowned and gave me a quick shake of her head to tell me Wynter was exaggerating, taking all the blame herself.

"I heard the lynx," Wynter continued. "I knew the guys would be out there, and we—"

Lisa held up her hand in front of Wynter's face and talked back to my mom.

"She wouldn't have even thought to go out there if your son wasn't sticking his nose into warden business—"

"Sticking my nose in?" Now I was spitting mad! "This is my land! And I don't play at being a game warden—I'm training to be one! Just ask Warden Kate. She teaches me things all the time!"

Mom put a hand on my shoulder to quiet me. "Wildlife is my son's passion. It's his interest. I'm not holding him back from that. Ever."

Lisa harrumphed. "A warden's job is very dangerous! Especially when it involves poaching! I'm warning you; he'll end up in trouble one day if you don't rein him in from these so-called adventures. I know. Firsthand!"

Wynter winced at her mom's words.

"Next time, he might—" Lisa cut herself off and waved a hand in the air dismissively. "Forget it. You wouldn't—you couldn't understand."

"You'd be surprised, Lisa." Mom's voice was steely. "I do understand. We've been there as a family." Mom caught my eye, and I knew she was remembering the time a tree fell on my dad, and the time Molly almost drowned.

Lisa looked hard at my mom. Putting a hand on the doorknob, she turned away. "Let's go, Wynter."

"Mom, please let me stay to hear what the wardens say—"

"Now!"

Wynter mouthed the word *Sorry* to me. I heard her pleading with her mom as she shut the door. "Can I at least stay overnight in the fort? I can't desert Summer now . . ."

My mom put an arm around me.

"Lisa isn't all wrong, you know." She pointed out the window to where Warden Kate and Warden Penny were watching the policeman put the poacher in his car. "He could have chased you all. Hurt you."

"We just needed to see why the lynx kitten was crying out," Packrat said.

"If we'd known a poacher was out there, too, we wouldn't have gone," Roy explained.

"I feel bad Wynter's mom is so mad about everything," Summer said sadly.

Mom's tired smile touched us all. "Everything worked out okay. This time."

Seeing the warden waving for us to join her, Mom opened the door and we all rushed across the driveway. I made a beeline for the trap and peeked inside.

No lynx.

"We apprehended this poacher by the trap," the warden explained. "Penny approached from a different direction in case he made a run for it. But I'm afraid the lynx you reported was nowhere to be found. This guy swears he's working alone and found the cage empty." She looked at us all. "You're sure the lynx was in the trap when you left?"

"Yes!" Summer, Roy, Packrat, and I said as one.

"Then somehow, it managed to escape before the poacher arrived. There was some blood." At my gasp, the warden reassured me. "Its tracks in the snow showed the bleeding was slight."

"Do you think it's hurt badly?" I asked.

"Lynx are pretty clever." Warden Kate's smile reassured me a bit. With a nod to Warden Penny, the two of them picked up the trap they had brought out of the woods and set it in the bed of the truck. "Want to take a closer look?"

Packrat, Roy, Summer, and I moved closer to the trap. We didn't touch the box because it was evidence. But we did lean in around it to get a better look.

There was no doubt about it: I could tell this was a permanent trap, made to sit in the same spot season after season because it'd be too heavy and bulky to lug all over the place. Inside against the back wall lay the bait; a snowshoe hare leg. I clenched my fists. How long had this trap been in my woods?

The box looked like a little log house, every log notched on either end so the one above it sat inside the grooves. The top and bottom were made of chicken wire, the door made from wooden slats. This poacher obviously didn't follow regulations when making his trap!

"Look!" I pointed to the top left corner where the chicken wire had pulled away six inches in either direction. And hanging off it was the lynx's collar! Three large tufts of fur were stuck to the wire next to it, too. I noticed a pinkish-red color on them. Blood?

Did the poor thing struggle?

"You've told me before," I said to the warden, "how lynx are calm when caught in a trap. But maybe this one tried to crawl out the hole between the wood and the wire?"

Summer gasped. "If it pushed with its paws or poked at the wire, it could have cut itself."

"The hole's kind of small, though. It couldn't have escaped that way," Roy pointed out.

"Maybe the poacher guy lied," Packrat suggested. "Maybe he did try to take the kitten out, and it got away from him. It'd be harder to hold onto without a collar."

Getting a little closer, I inspected the door. "This is the kind of trap that's set to wait until the animal gets inside and it accidentally steps on a release button, which drops the door."

"Very good!" Warden Kate said.

Suddenly, the whole scene unfolded in my mind.

"I've got it! I bet the kitten smelled the midnight snack." I pointed to the bait inside. "Once it stepped in, its paw hit the mechanism, dropping the door and trapping it. The lynx kitten moved around the cage, looking for a way out."

"The adult must have been outside," Packrat said.

"The kitten could have tried to see the adult out of the top of the cage and then got its collar caught on the wire. It struggled, and somehow it slipped from its collar and hurt its paw in the process."

"And the open door?" Packrat wondered.

"The cage was too heavy to fall over easily." This part wasn't as clear in my mind.

"But it was kind of tippy," Roy reminded me. "Like it was put down on a rock or a big stick or something. I had to hold it for you."

"So, when the kitten's collar got caught and it tried to free itself, maybe the cage tipped over," Packrat suggested.

"Or the other lynx pushed it over," Roy said.

I clenched my fists, fighting between relief that the door had popped open for the lynx to get away, and anger to find this illegal trap on my family's land. I soooooo wanted to kick that stupid box! Jump on it! Take a chain saw to it!

Voices raised in frustration had us looking across the road. Wynter and her mom still stood together, arms waving, words flying. Wynter kept pointing toward us and then in the direction of our forts.

"I'll go see if I can help," Summer said.

Warden Kate lifted her tailgate and snapped it closed. "Cooper, you said something about running into a winter blind out there, too?"

Packrat, Roy, and I nodded like bobbleheads.

"We didn't find it," said the warden.

"It was there!" I insisted. "If you sat inside, you'd have a clear view of the trap."

The poacher's voice drifted across from the backseat of the police car. "I don't know what happened to that lynx. You can't charge me without proof!"

Warden Penny leaned over and told him to settle down.

I looked at the poacher again. Shaggy brown hair poked out from underneath his hat. Short and stocky, his hands in handcuffs, he looked crunched up in the backseat.

Warden Penny murmured something to him again, and the guy dropped his chin to his chest in a huff.

"Moooooom?" Molly's crackly voice came through her radio, along with a couple of coughs.

"Is she sick?" Warden Kate asked.

"I'm afraid so," Mom replied.

Warden Kate gave her a sympathetic look as she turned to leave.

Into the radio, Mom told Molly, "I'm coming, honey. Stay in bed."

"Go ahead, Mom," I told her. "We'll get the office lights and lock up for you."

"Thanks, Cooper." With a glance toward the cage in the back of Warden Kate's truck, she said, "I hope this is the end of the poaching story."

I didn't have the heart to tell her that somehow, I thought it might be only the beginning.

CHAPTER 14

Lynx prefer to hunt in woodlands with dense undercover vegetation like thickets and deadfalls. They can climb trees and swim.

At six o'clock in the morning, the sun wasn't quite up yet, but the early light was enough to wake me up.

Quietly unzipping the tent so as not to wake my sleeping friends, I slipped outside and zipped it shut again to leave the warm air in.

Warm air. *The thermometer!*

Unzipping the tent, I leaned in and glanced at it.

Forty-one degrees.

Not bad!

I put it back and zipped the tent shut again.

Turning, I almost tripped over my own two feet at the sight before me. Our campfire was roaring already! I could see two sets of footprints coming from the girls' snow fort to our wood pile, to the campfire and everywhere in between. On our picnic table sat a note under a pot of water.

Going into town with my mom to pick up shiners for the derby. Used your fire ring and wood. We'll be back in plenty of time for the derby—
Wynter (and Summer)
PS: Our fort was forty-three degrees this morning.

I smiled. How could I have come so close to letting Roy convince me Wynter and her mom were poaching?

Picking up the pot, I put it on the grate over the fire. She obviously loves the outdoors, like I do. She loves her dogs. I shook my head. Wynter and her mother couldn't be poachers. Roy was just annoyed with Wynter, ready to blame the person he was most mad at.

And right now, he was spitting mad at Wynter. Because Wynter was beating him at his own game.

I'd just finished making cocoa for me and Packrat and coffee for Roy when I heard the tent zipper.

"Just in time," I told Roy. "Coffee's hot."

Roy took the tumbler I held out and took a sip. "Not bad. Girls?"

Roy was a man of few words this early in the morning. But I knew what he meant. Before I could tell him about the campfire and the note, I heard the tent zipper again. A bleary-eyed Packrat poked his head out. Rubbing his eyes with his left fist, he yawned. "What'd I miss?"

"Here," I said, handing him his hot cocoa. "We've got to go set up for the fishing derby."

Roy grabbed the note off our table to read it. "Forty-three degrees," he muttered, crushing the note up into a ball and tossing it into the campfire.

Roy must have seen our thermometer before he came out. He sure did hate losing a bet!

I shook off the feeling of needing to do something to help the lynx kitten right this minute. Only time would tell if its paw would get better.

But how could I check on it? Lynx like to stay hidden. It wouldn't be easy.

I had to put it out of my mind for a while, as we needed to set up for the derby.

After breakfast, my friends and I headed to the workshop to get the golf cart and gather what we needed. I left Roy and Packrat to load our fishing gear, while I tiptoed into my own kitchen to pack lunch for later. Putting six ham and cheese sandwiches in my oversize lunchbox, along with some drinks and blueberry muffins, I turned to tiptoe out the way I'd come in.

Hearing Molly's coughing fit upstairs, I paused at the kitchen door. She called out to Mom in a raspy whine. Mom answered wearily, just before I heard her feet hit the floor and her slippers squeak all the way to Molly's room.

Poor Squirt. Poor Mom, too.

For the gazillionth time, I was thankful it wasn't me with the cough. That would not be a fun winter break.

Ten minutes later, I was sitting in the driver's seat of the golf cart, with Packrat in the passenger seat and Roy on the bench seat between us. My friends had loaded the cart with wood for a campfire and added our ice-fishing poles, tackle boxes, an auger to drill holes in the ice, and our snowshoes. On the floor between Packrat's feet sat a partially covered bait bucket full of two-inch-long, silver fish. Hopefully, those shiners would attract a ginormous large-mouth bass. Maybe even a first-place catch!

"Is Summer still your scorekeeper to measure the fish and keep track of what people catch?" Packrat asked.

"Yep."

I put my foot gently on the brake as we headed downhill on the plowed road. When I'd asked last week if she was sure she wanted to do it, because it would mean she wouldn't be able to enter the contest, she'd said she would do it "for me."

But she liked Packrat, right? So, what the heck had she meant by that? I bet she'd just wanted to help with campground chores so she could hang around him more.

I snuck a look at my friend, who was waving to some kids heading to the derby on foot, their arms full of gear. "See you there!" Packrat called as we passed.

He didn't look lovesick to me.

"I've got you beat this year, Roy," the tallest guy in the group called out. "Found a new copper jig for the end of my line. I'm going after the giant trout you let get away last summer!"

Roy's head swiveled so fast toward the guy, I was surprised it didn't come off! My friend's competitiveness was legendary.

"Good luck with that!" Roy said, turning his whole upper body to gesture from the back of the cart, almost knocking Packrat out. "I've got a secret weapon this year, too!"

Settling back between Packrat and me, Roy folded his arms as a grin spread across his face.

"Secret weapon?" Packrat raised an eyebrow.

Roy rubbed his hands together. "I used three weeks' allowance on a handmade, wooden lure painted pink, red, and white. It's called Trout Love."

Packrat and I shared a snicker. "Catching love?" Packrat teased.

If only it was that easy, I thought.

Roy frowned. "It means for the love of trout! The guy at the bait store says it never fails to land him a huge fish!" Roy stared at each of us in turn, daring us to laugh again. Sheesh! Our friend took his lures seriously.

Parking the golf cart near a giant fire ring on the snow-covered beach, we scrambled out to pile the wood next to it. With each armload I scanned our lakefront area to make sure we had everything. Dad had plowed a big, round skating area and a trail across the lake and back before having supper with Molly and Mom and leaving for his campground owners' conference. Having a few activities would keep people busy while they waited for their orange flags to pop!

My eyes landed on Summer. She stood with her clipboard by a wooden picnic table she'd swept free of snow, signing in anyone who planned to weigh their fish for a chance to win prizes. She laughed and joked with everyone signing up, offering them hot cocoa, coffee, s'mores, and donuts.

Packrat came to stand beside me. "Speaking of love," he said, clearing his throat awkwardly, "it's really, you know, sweet, of Summer to help run the derby, huh?"

Thankfully, I didn't have to answer, because she was already rushing over. I reached into the golf cart and handed her a paper bag.

"A present for me?" Her green eyes lit up.

Present? "No!" I practically shouted. I couldn't let her think that!

Summer held the bag away from herself with two fingers, afraid to open it now, while Packrat shot me a weird look.

I rushed to explain. "We owe you blueberry pancakes because you won the temperature bet, but I didn't know when we'd find time to do that, so I got you and Wynter some blueberry muffins."

I didn't even take a breath, I was so scared my best friend would think I was trying to steal Summer away right from under his nose.

"Oh!" Summer smiled again. "Thanks. I think." She shook her head. "So, should I add you three to my list?" She hovered her purple pen over her clipboard, an eyebrow raised. I could see she already had fifteen people signed up.

"Our names are the only names you need!" Roy dropped an armload of wood on the pile like an exclamation point.

Summer's laugh rang out and her eyes twinkled as she waggled her pen at Roy.

"You're not just competing against Packrat and Coop this time!"

A crowd of eight walked toward us. Behind them came a couple with a little boy, maybe five years old, dressed in a blue snowsuit.

Summer turned away to greet them.

"Roy, you'd better go claim our fishing spots," I said, handing him the auger from the back of the cart.

"I'm on it."

Roy fast-walked onto the snow-covered ice and headed off to the right.

Packrat and I followed with our tackle boxes and ten-gallon buckets full of ice-fishing gear. We'd come up with a plan of action last night: Roy would use the auger to drill us six holes. Two we'd fish in with our short poles; on the other four we'd place our traps with the orange flags.

As we followed Roy out onto the ice and through the people, I looked around the lake. Wow! It was a great turnout! The couple with the little boy had marked their fishing spot by setting up a tan, square tent. As they unfolded blue camp chairs, their son took off running across the ice. Shooting out his left foot, he went into a slide, much like stealing home plate. Standing up, he dusted himself off and turned around to do it again.

Another guy, maybe in his early twenties, ran back and forth across the ice claiming old, frozen-over holes by using the heel of his boot to kick out the thin ice, then putting a trap over it. He cleared three of them in five minutes before grabbing the rope to his red sled and taking it from hole to hole to bait the traps and set them. I didn't see an auger, which might be why he had to rush to claim the old holes.

We caught up with Roy, who'd already drilled three holes about eight feet apart near the end of a long skinny island.

Packrat took off his glove. Putting his hand in the bait bucket, he lifted out a little wiggly shiner and hooked it to the end of his fishing line. Tucking his hand in his armpit, he grinned. "That water's cold!"

Next, he dropped the hook and shiner in the hole. "X marks the spot!" he said, putting the X-shaped base of the trap directly over the hole. Pulling the orange flag over and down to the base, he hooked it there before heading to the next hole.

Nearby, Roy stood the auger up onto the ice. Holding the handle, he began turning it like a drill. Down, down, down into the ice it went, throwing splinters in all directions. I knew the minute he broke through, because the auger dropped a foot before Roy hauled it up and out of the hole he'd made.

"We've got twelve inches of ice pretty much everywhere," he called back to us.

Twelve inches. Enough to hold a car!

Unfolding my camp chair, I sat to put a shiner on my line with a non-lead sinker. Dropping them into the water, I sat back and hoped a hungry brown trout lingered down there somewhere.

"Looks like you guys are pros at this!" Karl stepped up beside me, bundled from head to toe. Shading my eyes against the sun behind him, I looked up.

"We're out here all the time," I told him.

Karl juggled his over-the-shoulder camp chair bag, almost dropping his tackle box, cooler, and fishing pole. "What's the biggest fish you ever caught ice-fishing on Pine Lake?" he asked.

I looked at Packrat. "The sixteen-inch brown trout?"

Packrat sighed wistfully. "Yeah." He smiled up at Karl. "We let that one go."

Karl's eyebrows went up. "So, the winning fish is still in here!"

Roy laughed. "Yeah, somewhere in this two-hundred-acre lake!"

Karl gave a big belly laugh. "I haven't ice-fished in quite a few years. I'm looking forward to it."

Hearing the roar of a snowmobile, I looked out to the middle of the lake. The yellow snowmobile from the other day was racing up the length of it at breakneck speed! It traveled so fast, everyone at the derby stopped to stare.

Approaching our area of the lake, it slowed to crawling speed. The driver stood up, hands on the handles, searching the crowd. I couldn't see his or her face because the black helmet had a tinted shield. Suddenly, the driver nodded once toward the crowd. At who? Whipping around, I searched but didn't see an answering nod or a wave.

Did I imagine it?

Revving up the machine, the driver sat and took off, flying back down the lake.

"Weird." Packrat echoed the thought in my head.

"Just trying to be cool," Roy scoffed.

I wasn't so sure.

Two hours later I'd caught two brown trout, one at fifteen inches, and another at fifteen and three-quarters. We decided to keep those fish, so whichever one of us lost today could cook them up for supper. My stomach rumbled at the thought of trout roasting over the campfire with onions and red peppers.

Roy hadn't caught anything with his secret-weapon lure, and Packrat teased him a ton.

"You know," Roy said, glancing toward Karl, who was still fishing by his hole nearby, "I think he just put a fourth fish in his cooler. And it didn't look no fourteen inches to me. Neither did the last one he caught."

"Maybe he forgot the rules?" I wondered. Karl wasn't from Maine, so even though he needed a license to fish, he might not have read the book on fishing limits. "I wouldn't want Warden Kate to show up and catch him with the wrong amounts."

One of Karl's flags popped up. He race-walked over, moved the trap, and pulled up the line until the fish lay on the ice, wiggling and slapping its tail down. From where I sat, it looked like an eight-incher. Karl stared down at it longer than he needed to.

"Get out your tape measure. Get out your tape measure," I muttered.

Karl gazed over the derby, taking everything in. I ducked my head, while Roy studied the trap closest to him, and Packrat pretended to tie the laces on his boot. Crouching down next to the fish, Karl picked it up. I held my breath. He wouldn't!

Plop! Into his cooler it went.

I stood up. Customer service or not, I had to tell him.

"Finally!" Roy cried, as his fishing pole bent downward again.

Then my flag popped!

I ran to my trap and picked it up. Turning the reel, I brought my catch up, up, up!

Packrat had run to help Roy. Pulling a tape measure from his coat pocket, he held it up to the fish's snout, measuring all the way to the top of the tail. "Nice one!" Reading the number, he whistled low. "Seventeen inches!"

"Hey, Summer!" Roy put both hands around his mouth and called out to where she stood near the shoreline. "We got one!"

"Coming!" she called back.

Packrat took a few running steps, then slid over to me to measure mine. "It's bigger than Roy's!" he said, pulling out his tape.

"Coooooooper!" Summer's voice sounded weirdly off. Dropping my fish, still on its line, into the hole, I searched for her among the crowd.

On the ice, just off a jut of land at the end of the beach, Summer pointed to a patch of open water across a narrow bit of lake. Practically jumping up and down, she waved her arm to get my attention, pointing frantically toward the open water where an eagle flapped its wings on the surface as if trying to stay afloat.

Roy joined me and Packrat. "Eagles swim?"

I shook my head. "Not on purpose they don't."

Packrat already had binoculars to his eyes. "I can't tell. The water's too deep there for it to be bathing!"

Summer pointed toward the eagle again. Dropping her clipboard, she started walking toward it. Even though she was a good fifty feet from the patch of open water, my blood froze.

"Summer! Wait—don't! There's a current under there!"

I took off running.

"Summer! Thin ice! Come back!" the three of us called.

I didn't know if Summer couldn't hear us, or if she was just so curious about the eagle, she'd tuned us out.

Finally, she turned around. She looked down. She looked back at us. Her eyes widened as they met mine. I held up my hand: *Stop!*

The eagle cried out once, twice.

Summer's hands went up as she fell through the ice.

The three of us broke into a full run.

CHAPTER 15

Lynx will hide food for later; the food storage spot is called a cache.

"Summer!"

She'd only fallen through the ice up to her thighs, but there wasn't time to breathe a sigh of relief. Her wide hazel eyes were locked onto mine, pleading silently for help.

I knew she now stood on another layer of ice, but that layer was probably thin too!

Leaning forward, Summer tried to pull herself out, but the ice broke off more.

"Don't move!" I cried.

Startled, she looked at me again.

"Stay still!" I instructed. Seeing her shake from head to toe, I added, "Trust me."

"I trust you," she mouthed back. Even from this distance, I could see her shivering lips. She had to be freezing.

When there's a frigid cold wave and temps go up to, say, forty-five or fifty degrees, and then plummet back down to freezing temperatures again, weak spots sometimes form on the lake, with water between two layers of ice. Add a moving water current underneath it all, and you end up with a dangerous situation like this one.

Packrat and I had almost reached her. I heard someone call my name, once, twice, but I didn't stop to find out who, or why. If we didn't hurry, the second layer of ice could break under Summer too, or at the very least, she'd get hypothermia.

Packrat pulled a thick, light blue climbing rope from his pocket.

"Stop here!" I told him.

We laid down on the ice and crawled closer still, spreading our weight out so we wouldn't fall through. We weren't even close, but if we fell in, it wouldn't help her at all.

Seeing us, Summer reached out as far as she could, eager to free herself.

"No!" I cried. "Be patient."

I heard people behind us, arguing. Summer was all I saw.

Packrat tossed the rope to her, groaning when it fell halfway. Dragging it back, he balled it up in his hand to try again.

"Wait!" I had an idea. "The rope needs weight on the end."

Without a word, he pulled a small hammer from an outside pocket. With a quick knot, he tied it on the end and tossed again. This time the rope landed on the ice and slid within six inches of Summer's hand.

"Careful, go slow," I cautioned when Summer reached out eagerly. Wrapping her pointer finger around the handle, she tugged it closer until she could grab it with her whole hand and pull the rope toward her. Once she had it, she wound the rope around the palm of her right hand, then grabbed a hunk of the rest with her left.

Now I allowed myself to breathe a small sigh of relief. At least we had her if the ice below broke. And not a minute too soon; I swear her lips were turning blue!

"We're gonna pull you up and out! Lie on your stomach like us!"

Summer nodded. Her whole body shivered, from fear or the cold, I wasn't sure. Maybe both.

I swallowed, my heart practically beating out of my chest. This had to work!

Packrat and I pulled the rope. Summer came up and out of the hole onto her stomach just like we'd told her to. Right away, I noticed her jeans were dripping wet from her thighs down. Water ran out of the tops of her boots onto the ice. I sympathy-shivered.

Once we'd dragged her a few feet from the hole, Packrat and I stopped pulling and scooted backward on the ice, still lying down. We pulled her in some more.

Someone lifted my boots and pulled me backward quickly, taking Summer, too. Packrat slid with me. Back on thicker ice, I rolled over to find Roy looking down at me. His face grim, he held out a hand to help me up. I shook my head. "Get Summer!"

"Wynter's mom has her," he said, pointing behind me. Lisa had already helped Summer up and was wrapping her in a blanket.

"Sorry I didn't get out there to help you guys," he said, as I took his hand and he pulled me to my feet. "I had to hold back Lisa and Karl. She got spitting mad when you ran ahead and didn't listen when she called you back." Roy glanced at Wynter, who was pulling Packrat up.

"I didn't hear her," I said, not taking my eyes off Summer.

"Karl finally showed up and he told her to let you go. You were doing everything right."

Summer was shivering as Lisa looked her over.

"Can you walk?" Lisa asked gently. Summer nodded.

"I'm taking you home." Lisa's voice left no room for arguing. "Wynter," she hollered, "start the truck!" Wynter took off running.

Lisa caught my eye and her worried face changed instantly to a steely look. Geez! Couldn't I do anything right? She steered Summer away from us, speaking soothingly. "We'll get you home and out of those clothes—"

"The eagle!" Summer whirled to look back from where she'd come.

There, sitting on the edge of the ice with a twenty-inch lake trout, sat the eagle. It looked at us regally as if to say *What's all the fuss?*

I shook my head. "Looks like it grabbed a fish too big to fly off with. What you saw, Summer, was the eagle swimming its catch to shore."

Summer laughed, even as her teeth chattered. "I think it gets the w-win for t-today."

"C'mon now." Lisa turned her around to get to her truck. A murmuring crowd parted for them. Wynter stood on the shoreline, her mom's truck running and waiting.

Everyone headed back to their fishing holes.

Karl walked back with us. "You were off and running before I could figure out what was happening. Great job, Cooper."

Honestly, I was still shaking in my boots. If Summer had fallen all the way through—my heart skipped a beat at the nightmare thought.

Someone had added wood to the fire on the beach. The sun hung just above the treetops. The family with the five-year-old boy had begun packing up. I hoped he'd caught something, even if it was small.

"I'm done for today," I said. "I've got my limit of two."

"Yeah, I'll pack up, too." Suddenly, Roy stood tall. He raised his chin and looked down at us regally. "Since I had the biggest fish today, I'm the King of the Lake! And you two are cooking! I like my fish sautéed in butter, garlic, and onions. I'll take a side of home fries and macaroni salad. And I'd better see blueberry pie for dessert."

"You'll get what you cooked for us when you lost. Fish cooked in tin foil with onions, and a cookie for dessert, Your Highness," Packrat

teased, as he opened our cooler. He blinked, closed the lid, looked at Roy and me, then lifted the lid again.

"What's wrong?" I asked, pulling up my trap and line.

"Isn't this our fish cooler?"

"Yeah."

"No fish."

"What?" Roy flew over, sliding to a stop in front of the cooler. "What the heck?" he cried, seeing it empty.

I looked around. Who would have taken our fish? Whoever it was, they did it while we were saving Summer.

Roy said he'd had to hold Lisa back. Where had Wynter been? And Karl?

I glanced his way to find him staring into his own cooler with a funny look. "My fish is gone," he said, scratching his head through his hat.

The three of us headed over. "Ours, too!" I told him.

Karl sighed and lowered his lid before we got there. "Well, I hope whoever took them needs the food more than we do."

Roy scowled; his fists clenched and unclenched. I didn't want him to be grumpy at our campfire.

"We can catch more tomorrow," I said.

"It's the idea of it!" he spat out. "Besides, I was looking forward to you two treating me like a king and all."

"Me, too," I assured him. "Well, the eating fish part. Not treating you like a king."

Packrat chimed in, saying quietly, "I just, you know, gotta wonder why."

By the time we'd packed up our gear and gotten to the beach, everyone had gathered near the fire to hear the results of the derby. I grabbed Summer's clipboard from the table and quickly scanned her notes with a sigh. Poor Summer. She'd been so excited to give out the awards.

I heard chatter on how the biggest catch of the day was the eagle's, and laughter when someone mentioned it was disqualified from taking first place because it hadn't officially registered with Summer.

Third place went to the little boy for catching a sixteen-inch trout. The kid had been hugging it for an hour, as if it was a stuffed animal, and he refused to let it go.

The second-place red ribbon went to Roy. I kidded him, insisting that at next year's derby, the use of Trout Love lures would be banned.

"Don't you dare!" he growled, punching my shoulder playfully.

First place went to the twenty-something guy who'd opened the old holes. When I called out his name from Summer's clipboard to present him with free passes to the Whittier Wildlife Center, he stepped forward shyly as everyone clapped.

Karl had been packing up his stuff quickly. I saw him walking away from the crowd without a backward glance. I bet he was wicked mad that someone had taken his fish. I couldn't blame him.

With the last of the awards given out, I turned in a circle to scan the crowd.

People stood around in small groups, chatting and comparing fish-that-got-away stories. It felt really good to know that everyone had had a good time. I couldn't wait to tell Dad!

Except, I thought, someone out there was a fish thief.

But who? And why?

CHAPTER 16

Lynx have a good sense of smell, but they rely more on their eyesight and hearing when hunting.

Dusk had arrived, and with it, ice fog. Wisps of it floated a couple of feet above the ice, giving our surroundings an eerie, horror-movie feel. Yet, it looked beautiful, too.

The eagle, who'd eaten its big catch of the day on a fallen tree trunk by the open water, now perched on a branch above our heads only a hundred or so feet away. It had hung out there after preening, watching us clean a couple of trout a camper had given us after learning that ours had been stolen.

"Greedy raptor!" Roy had called out to it. He sat with his feet up, watching us prepare the fish to cook. "One of you needs to put some fish parts out there for it." And because Packrat and I had lost the bet, we'd done it. Along with a bunch of other chores he'd ordered us to do. So far, the eagle hadn't taken the bait, but Roy sure had ordered us around a ton.

We were the last three at the lakeside fire now, and I stifled a yawn as I picked up our supper dishes and put them in a plastic bin.

"Hey." Roy pointed to a fork on the picnic table right next to him. "You forgot one."

"Bring it—"

Roy lifted a finger and waggled it back and forth. "The bet was for me to be treated like a king. A king!"

"Kind of a bossy king, don't you think?" Packrat muttered loud enough for his words to reach the grinning Roy. But he went and got it. A bet's a bet!

"Cooper!" Roy whispered. "Freeze!"

His hushed voice told me something interesting was close by. Turning slowly, I scanned the edge of the woods.

The lynx kitten!

It took a cautious step out into the open and sniffed the air before taking another step. It must not have seen us in the dusk.

I waved a hand toward the ground. We all crouched low.

"It's limping a bit."

Probably from the cut in its paw, I thought.

"Is it me, or is it skinnier than the first time we saw it?" Packrat asked sadly.

Roy looked around. "I wish we had something more to give it."

The lynx silently crept over to the golf cart.

"It smells the fish we cooked!" I whispered.

Its nose twitching in the air, the lynx put its huge front paws on the back of the golf cart bed to sniff around the pan. We held our breath when it jumped back down and sniffed the air again. This time, its nose led it right to the fish parts we'd thrown out for the eagle.

"It must be really hungry," I told my friends as it wolfed down what little was there. "Fish isn't high on its list of favorite foods."

The eagle shook all over, ruffling its feathers as if annoyed with the lynx. Spreading its wings, it lifted off and soared away.

Headlights shone through the trees as a vehicle came down the camp road. The three of us turned to check it out and when we looked back, the lynx had gone.

I sighed. "Well," I said as I stood, "at least it got something to eat today."

Warden Kate's truck came into view. Parking near the golf cart, she stepped out and headed over to us. "I heard about Summer," she said as she joined us. "Quick thinking! Thank goodness the second layer of ice held her."

She held her hands out over the campfire flames. "So, Cooper, remember when you said one of your goals this vacation was to take a trip to Piehl Mountain? Were you thinking of visiting the Hercules crash site?"

This Warden Kate was all business, not friendly, curious Warden Kate. "Yeah."

"Don't go."

I frowned, because I'd been looking forward to it. "Why not?"

Warden Kate stared into the flames like she was deciding something. We stayed quiet, letting her think. Finally, she put her hands in her pockets.

"What I say here must stay here, okay? Only you and Warden Penny will know." She looked us each in the eye, one by one, and we nodded our solemn oath.

"We had to let the poacher, Thomas Scott, go today."

The three of us began protesting, talking over each other, asking questions. The warden held up a hand.

"Let me finish. He had his hearing before a judge and he's out on bail until the trial. He's being charged with poaching and trespassing, but honestly, the poaching charge might not stand. We didn't get him with the lynx. We searched his residence, and I didn't find any signs of trapping, pelts, or wildlife parts. You wouldn't even know the guy hunted at all."

My heart sank. "So, this Thomas Scott guy is just gonna get away with it?"

The warden's mouth moved upward slightly. "Maybe not. We got an anonymous tip, leading me to believe he's someone we've been looking for, for quite a while. Someone who collects three and four times as many pelts than they should every season."

"How can he trap that many animals but no one sees him or has proof?" Packrat cried.

"That's the thing. Coming here to catch the lynx? With all the campers you have right now? I don't think it's his normal mode of operation," Warden Kate said. "It's too public." She tapped the fire ring with her boot, making the embers shift and settle. Little flames popped up here and there. "I think your family opening the campground in winter this year for the first time took him by surprise, but he risked trapping here anyway because someone told him this particular lynx kitten made an easy target. And I bet he was paid exceptionally well to take the chance."

The warden looked off down the lake toward the old bridge. "No, the tip I got said he has a base in a remote place deep in the woods— he's got to have some sort of shelter—a place where he can take all the pelts he wants, and no one notices. And I believe it."

It all came together for me. "You think his base is near the Hercules plane crash site on Piehl Mountain?"

The warden nodded. "This person also mentioned that Thomas Scott sells his pelts to someone who takes them to Canada to resell."

At those last words, Roy stiffened and shot me an aha look.

"That way, no one here can put two and two together. Also, I believe he has a ton of pelts right now which he's secretly and quickly trying to unload before his trial. I'm heading into that area before first light tomorrow to check it out and hopefully get the proof we need. So, I'd like you to stay put right here on your own trails while I find his camp and stake it out."

"A stakeout?" Roy grinned. "In the middle of the woods in winter?"

Packrat looked up and down at the warden's hunter-green uniform. "Won't you stand out like a red fox on a white field?"

Warden Kate smiled. "No worries. I have a full winter camouflage suit." Her smile got wider. "I've had animals walk ten feet away from me and not notice I was standing there."

"Whoa!" I breathed. *The possibilities!*

"Can you show us your winter gear sometime?" Packrat asked.

"Sure, as soon as this case is done. I promise."

Thinking about Warden Kate, all alone in a remote area of woods, staking out a poacher, had me a little worried. "You're taking Warden Penny for backup, right?"

Putting a hand on my shoulder, she focused on me intently. "Penny is staying to take care of other things. I'm trained to do this. I'll be back in eighteen hours, tops, and I'll call." To all of us, she added, "I'm breaking every rule in my book by telling you three this information, but I believe you deserve an explanation about why the poacher got released, and why I'm asking you to stay here.

"If you need anything or see anything suspicious while I'm gone, let Penny know. She's familiar with the territory, more than I realized. You can trust her." The warden winked. "Besides, if I'm on a stakeout, my phone has to be off, you know."

The dark night had slipped in around us. The moon, mostly full, peeked up over the trees at the end of the lake. Cold seeped into my winter suit from the feet up. I wiggled my toes in my heavy socks.

The warden said her good-byes and got back in her truck.

I poured water over the embers, hearing the sizzle as the fire went out completely.

"So, if the poacher is free for now," I wondered aloud, "do you suppose he's still after the lynx?"

Packrat nodded. "He'd want to finish the job."

"That kitten is hurt and hungry." Roy couldn't meet my eyes. "I don't know if it stands a chance."

I silently vowed to keep the lynx kitten safe until Warden Kate reported back to us. Safe from Thomas Scott. Safe from whoever had paid him to trap it. And safe from hunger, too.

CHAPTER 17

Male lynx are territorial, living alone most of the time.

"So what exactly is this Hercules crash place Warden Kate talked about?" Roy asked, as we settled into the bedroom in Packrat's camper.

With two bunks on one side and two more on the other wall, we had to stand sideways and move around one at a time in order to get in and out of the skinny room. When we were little, it wasn't so bad. In fact, we'd had some epic pillow fights without even leaving our bunks! But now that we were all grown up, it was a tight fit.

We'd thought about sleeping at my house, but Molly was still sick, and none of us wanted to risk catching her cold. Then we thought about sleeping in our fort again, but after being outside all day, the damp cold had seeped into our bones, and we really needed to warm up. So, the bunks would have to do. Packrat's mom, who slept in the master bedroom at the other end of the camper, was happy to have us, as long as we weren't too loud.

"It's a really cool, historic memorial on Piehl Mountain where a C-130 Hercules plane crashed over fifty years ago during a sudden nor'easter." I hung down from my top bunk while explaining to Packrat and Roy, who lay on their backs looking up at me from their bottom bunks.

"Was it carrying people?" Packrat asked.

"It had a crew of three." I tried to remember all the details from the historical sign my mom and I had read when we'd visited two summers ago. "The Hercules was a military plane and it could transport troops or cargo. This time, it carried three pilots and a troop of five. Nobody survived. That's why it's a memorial site now."

"Military!" Roy rolled up onto one elbow. "Was it on a fighter mission?"

"No, it was transporting the men and supplies from one base to another. Some of the pieces of the wreckage are huge—like the tires! And other pieces are small."

Packrat yawned so big, he hiccupped. "How far away is it?"

"By car, you'd have to travel roads around the lake and then up the mountain onto some dirt roads. You park in a mini parking lot, then ride an ATV or snowmobile or hike over an all-purpose trail to get to it. In the winter, if you follow our lake to the end, you can hop right on the all-purpose trail and save a lot of time. It's a really long, all-day hike, but it can be done."

"But you heard Warden Kate," I said, rolling onto my back to put my head on my pillow. "We've got to steer clear of it."

"Yeah," Packrat said wistfully from his bottom bunk across from me.

"Whatever," Roy replied from his bunk below.

The room was mostly dark. Moonlight from the full moon shone through two small rectangular windows on my side of the camper. "The warden said she'd be back late tomorrow. So maybe we can go to the crash site later in the week. Besides, there's other things we can do while we wait," I suggested. "Like dogsledding on Wednesday."

"Dogsledding." I heard Roy roll over. "Give me a snowmobile any day."

"Eh, eya quant ta tee nit." This was Packrat's half-asleep answer for wanting to try it.

I shrugged. "I think it'll be fun."

Heavy breathing signaled to me that both my friends had fallen asleep.

Pulling the blankets up to my ears, I stared out the little window into the woods beyond. Where was the lynx now? What if the person who stole the fish today tried using them as bait? I wished for the gazillionth time I could get close enough to make sure the kitten's paw wasn't getting infected.

I rolled over restlessly. Who was I kidding? I'd never get close enough to a lynx. Without gear like Warden Kate's, it would see me coming a mile away and—

That's it!

I sat straight up and BANG! My head slammed into the ceiling.

"Owww!" I cried. I'd forgotten how low the ceilings are in a camper.

Sssnnnnzzzzt! Packrat snored loudly, then burrowed deeper into his sleeping bag while Roy threw an arm over his eyes. Should I wake them?

Nah. It'd been a long day. I could fill them in on my idea tomorrow.

Feeling better, knowing I had a plan to stake out the little lynx, I rolled back over and stared out into the woods outside until my eyes got heavy, and I drifted off to sleep.

The next morning, I told Packrat and Roy my great idea over breakfast in Packrat's camper.

"We can make our own camouflage suits!"

Roy scowled into his bowl of cereal. "You know I'm no good at crafty stuff."

"It's okay." I figured he'd say that. "While Packrat and I make them, you can catch a couple of fish."

Roy's face brightened. "I'm on it!" He picked up his bowl to drink the rest of his milk and cereal in one gulp. Standing, he shrugged into his coat. "Later, guys."

Packrat picked up his bowl and Roy's and took them to the sink to wash them. "So, where do we start?" he asked.

I grabbed my coat and boots. "All we need are some white ponchos with hoods, some brown and black spray paint, and black pants to help hide us."

"White ponchos? Where the heck are you gonna find those?" Packrat held the camper door open for me. "We're leaving, Mom!" he called back toward her bedroom.

"I'll be in the store today!" she replied. "Molly's still sick."

"Got it!" he said, closing the door.

"The store is where we're headed, too," I told him.

Twenty minutes later, Packrat and I stepped back onto his site after grabbing all the white ponchos in the camp store and leaving Mom a note.

Suddenly Summer appeared, a grin on her face.

"Found you!" She threw her arms wide. "I've been looking all over! I need to thank you."

Before I could think about it, she'd wrapped her arms around me, put her head on my shoulder, and squeezed tight. Not sure what to do, I patted her shoulder awkwardly. "Yeah. No problem."

"No problem?" she said, stepping back. "You saved me from certain death!"

Packrat stepped away from us. I grabbed his arm and dragged him back. I didn't want to get between him and Summer. "I would have done the same for anybody. Besides, Packrat here," I clapped him on the back, "did most of the saving. He had the rope and all. Really. You should be thanking him."

Summer hesitated. "But you . . ." Shrugging, she leaned into Packrat and hugged him tight, making his ears turn red.

Stepping back, she tilted her head to the side, studying the two of us. "So, what are you guys up to today?"

I hesitated. I didn't want to lie. Especially now when I could still feel her hug. But what if Roy was right about Wynter? Or her mom? They were from Canada, and Warden Kate said the person who wanted to buy the pelts came from Canada. And then there was the promise we'd made to Warden Kate; she'd told us about the Canada stuff in confidence. I decided to tell a half-truth.

"We're winter-camouflaging ourselves."

Summer's face lit up. "You must be going after the lynx! Can I help?"

Normally, I'd have said yes, and then filled Summer in on everything. No holding back. But she was spending tons of time with Wynter, choosing her over us—twice now!

I cleared my throat while sliding my handful of ponchos behind my back. "We don't have enough."

Summer's smile dropped. Her eyes narrowed. I instantly felt terrible. Her hands balled into fists. She took a step toward me. I took a step back.

"What you mean," she said, her words low and measured, "is that you don't want Wynter and me tagging along. Why?"

"Well, she's a . . ." I looked to Packrat.

"Don't look at him!" Summer cried. "I want to know why."

"She's a . . . suspect?" I framed it like a question.

Summer's hands punched the air above her. "Of all the crazy boy ideas I've ever heard!"

"C'mon," Packrat put a hand on her arm. "Don't fight. We've only got a few days left to hang out together."

Summer relaxed a bit, giving Packrat a grateful look. "You're right. I don't want to waste our vacation time being mad," she agreed. "Besides, the warden's caught the poacher. So . . ."

"Umm, yeah," I said weakly, while Packrat nodded like a bobblehead.

Summer's gaze whipped over to me again.

I focused on giving her my best trying-not-to-give-anything-away look, but her eyes narrowed.

"You know something else," she breathed. When Packrat and I didn't deny it, she backed away. "Wynter is giving dogsled rides tomorrow. It's easily the coolest activity you have this week. Why would she do it if she were looking to take a lynx off your property? Huh?"

"To distract us," I said quietly.

Summer shook her head. "Nope. I don't believe it. If she can't help, I'm not helping either." She folded her arms.

"C'mon, Summer," I said. "I think Wynter is cool, too. But her mom . . ."

Summer's angry face went sad. Giving us one last look, she said, "You can't judge Wynter based on her mom. I'll find a way to prove it to you. She's not who you think she is."

Then Summer walked off Packrat's campsite without a backward glance.

CHAPTER 18

A lynx can spot a mouse 250 feet away.

Packrat and I hung the ponchos outside to spray-paint random black and brown marks on them. I thought they looked like birch trees from a distance. I hoped they worked!

Roy came back to our campsite an hour later with two brown trout. "This is all I got," he said. But his squared shoulders and proud smile told us he knew they were perfect.

Wearing black snow pants over our jeans, we pulled the ponchos over our heads and raised the hoods to cover our hair.

"Am I invisible yet?" Packrat joked.

"Where's that voice coming from?" I asked while pulling on black gloves. "Roy? Did you hear something?"

Roy turned in a circle, his poncho swirling out around his knees. "Someone's playing tricks."

Packrat rolled his eyes at us. "Let's hope the lynx is more fooled than you two."

By now it was barely noon, and I knew the sun would set around five o'clock or so. "Let's go," I said.

We chose the spot where the lynx had been trapped, for two reasons. One, the kitten had already found food there. And two, we'd be able to blend into the grouping of young birch trees where we'd found the blind.

Roy threw the fish out into the snow about thirty to forty feet away before coming back to kneel down among the trees with us. "I hope the lynx finds it."

Packrat's hand came out from under his poncho. In it he held a small camera. He then pulled out a three-foot-high tripod and attached the camera to the top of it. Looking through the viewfinder, he put the fish in the frame.

"But if you move to hit the button," Roy said, "you'll scare the lynx kitten off."

Packrat pulled out a remote control and raised an eyebrow.

"Shoulda known," I said.

We sat against the trees in silence for a few minutes. Finally, Roy whispered, "This is gonna take a while, isn't it?"

I shifted a bit and shrugged. "If the lynx was totally wild, I don't think we'd see it at all. But if what we suspect is true, if somebody dumped the kitten on our land because they couldn't take care of it or control it—"

"It means the kitten is staying here because of the people and the food," Packrat finished for me.

I agreed. "It'll come by."

Another forty minutes, and my eyes were getting droopy. So far, my friends and I had only seen a pileated woodpecker, its long, strong beak rat-a-tat-tatting against a rotted log, hoping for a lunch of ant and beetle larvae, and a clever crow who I swear had figured out we were in disguise. It flew into the forest hollering caw-caw to announce itself. I hoped the lynx didn't understand raven talk.

We almost missed the porcupine; it was so quiet compared to the other two. Backing down the trunk of a nearby hemlock, it waddled right past us, looking for its next dining spot. Seeing it reminded me of Karl and his mascot, Petunia.

The porcupine stopped near a hemlock branch lying on top of the snow. Standing on its hind legs, the animal held the branch in its little hands to eat every bit of green off of it before dropping it and continuing on its way.

By now my right foot felt prickly from kneeling so long in the same position. I wiggled my foot, but it only made it prickle more. Putting a hand to the ground, I started to stand.

"Wait!" Packrat cautioned. "Hear that?"

Roy stiffened and sucked in a breath.

Crunching sounds—footsteps in the snow—floated toward us through the woods. I tried to move only my eyes, not my head. My heart started beating double time.

A flash of purple off to the right, then blue, then bright green! Voices now, hushed, two of them.

"People," I cautioned.

"Let's stay put," Roy suggested.

"Yeah! We'll test the camouflage," Packrat agreed.

We stayed as still as we could. The voices got louder. Louder still.

"Wait. A. Minute." Roy's soft voice held a rumble of annoyance. "I know those voices."

Summer and Wynter.

Packrat started to stand, but this time Roy urged him to stay put. "Maybe I'll get a clue on her middle name!"

It felt wrong to listen in on our friends' conversation. But I went along with it, hoping the girls would say something to prove Roy wrong about Wynter and Lisa being suspects.

"Here!" Summer walked with high steps, talking to Wynter over her shoulder. The two of them wore snowshoes and held a trekking pole in each hand. Summer stopped to point with her right pole at something on the ground. "Look! Lynx tracks again. It doubled back."

Roy raised an eyebrow and gave me a pointed look.

"So what?" I shrugged. "They're just doing what we're doing."

"With all the talking, they'll never see it," Roy grumbled.

I had to admit, he was right about that.

So far, the girls hadn't spied us. I was glad to see they didn't have Moose or Raven with them; the dogs would have ratted us out for sure, even with our camouflage.

Stopping to catch their breath, they scanned the woods while leaning on their poles.

"Soooooo," Wynter said, a smile forming across her face, "have you tried to get his attention yet, like I told you?"

I glanced at Packrat, but he was busy watching his fingers as he rolled a hunk of poncho around. Roy caught my look and frowned. Did he know Packrat liked her?

Summer took a sudden interest in chopping the snow by her boot with her trekking pole. "Yeah, but you know boys. They're weird. You could hit them over the head with a fish and they wouldn't notice you."

What was she talking about? We hung out together all the time! *Unless*, I had a sudden thought, *what if Packrat was too shy to tell her he liked her back?*

The girls snowshoed on, in and out of our sight, moving through the trees.

Wynter shrugged. "Speaking of weird boys, tell me," Wynter asked, "what's Roy's deal?"

Roy stiffened. For a second, I thought he'd charge out of his hiding spot to ask Wynter what the heck she was talking about.

"What do you mean?" Summer asked.

"He's always so gloom and doom, you know."

Summer didn't say anything for a minute, but her steps slowed, until finally she stopped.

C'mon, Summer. I know you're mad at Roy, and me, but be nice! I wasn't sure what Roy would do if Summer said something mean. Or worse yet, if she told Wynter he thought she was a suspect.

Finally, Summer said, "It just takes him a while to get to know you. But once he does, he's a loyal friend for life."

Wynter seemed to consider her words for a minute. "Okay." She stepped in front of Summer. "I just need to try harder."

Summer giggled a little, while Roy groaned beside me.

"Try harder?" he grumbled. "Try harder at what? Driving me crazy? Making me mad?" he muttered. "Try harder. *Psssh.*"

"Hey," Summer said over her shoulder, "can I ask about you and your mom and camping out? You two sure go a lot of places. I wish my dad and I traveled like that. Do you come down from Canada a lot?"

"Sure." Wynter shrugged, not offering any more info.

Looked like Summer had struck out. Couldn't blame her for trying.

"So, what is your middle name, anyway?" Summer's voice faintly trailed back to us, as the girls' path took them down a small slope and out of sight.

Roy perked up. He turned his whole body toward them, leaning in, trying to catch the answer.

"Promise you won't tell?" Wynter said. "It's my grandmother's name, actually . . ."

Their voices faded. "No, no, no!" Roy slumped back to sit against a tree trunk.

"Well, it's a clue," I told him. "It must be an old name."

"It could be anything!" Roy threw his hands in the air, making his poncho wiggle around. "Oops," he said. "Right. Stay still. We're blending in."

After only five more minutes, a long, low rumbling sound filled the air around us. Packrat and I leaned away from Roy, looking at his stomach. Then the three of us burst into muffled laughter. Packrat fell over on his back from giggling so hard.

"A little hungry?" I looked at my watch. "Maybe we should head back. I don't think the lynx will come by with the girls out there—"

"Not come by," Packrat whisper-interrupted from the ground. "Come down."

"Come down?" Roy whispered.

Packrat lifted his arm to point about fifteen feet up into a huge, bare oak tree. There, lying on a branch, was our lynx!

"Has it been there the whole time?" I asked.

Roy snorted. "The girls walked right under it!"

The lynx lazily licked its injured paw over and over and over again, then licked the fur on its leg. Stretching and flexing, it stood on the branch to survey the area.

"Where's the adult?" I whispered.

Walking across the branch like a tightrope, the lynx went to the trunk and looked up. Stretching its big paws up and around the trunk, it then scrambled backwards down the tree. At about seven feet off the ground, it turned in one move to silently jump the rest of the way down.

The lynx stopped to lick its paw again before gazing into the woods around us. Ears turning to catch all the sounds, it approached the fish, then stopped. Getting low to the ground so its stomach almost touched the snow, the lynx took another couple of stalking steps.

Packrat got out the remote control for his camera. The lynx took four more steps, bringing it closer and closer. I could clearly make out the black on the end of its bobbed tail and the black tufts of hair standing straight up from the tips of its ears.

"Whoa," Packrat breathed.

Its legs were long and thick. Every time one of its snowshoe-like paws hit the ground, they spread out. The rest of the lynx seemed so very cat-like, right down to its white whiskers and the way it twitched its nose.

The lynx put out a paw and touched the fish. It circled it, walking around it, looking at it from all sides. Suddenly it leapt forward and grabbed the fish in its mouth. Whirling, it trotted toward us. I mean, right toward us! Twenty feet away. Fifteen feet away. I waited for it to see us, smell us. Ten feet away! Eight!

I jumped up. The lynx kitten stopped, its yellow eyes questioning. Crouching down, it kept the fish in its mouth. A low rumbling sound came from its throat. It backed up a step, never taking its eyes off me.

Click, click, click! Packrat's camera sounded wicked loud in the silence of the woods.

The lynx, not sure of the sound, backed up and crouched on its hind legs, ready to take off at the slightest hint of danger.

To my surprise, my hands began to shake. I could almost reach right out and feel how soft its fur was. But I didn't dare.

Suddenly, the lynx reared back, twisted, and took off running, its prize still in its mouth.

My knees gave out and I sat down weakly.

"I guess the ponchos work?" Packrat whispered.

"They work good," Roy replied.

A little too good, I thought.

CHAPTER 19

*Lynx whiskers are like fingers. Lynx move them with
their face muscles. The whiskers help lynx avoid objects
in the dark by feeling for them.*

I couldn't wait to report to Warden Kate on how well the camouflage
ponchos had worked—especially the fact that the lynx had come so
close, we were able to count its whiskers! Seventeen on each side, as a
matter of fact.

Remembering that Warden Kate had told us we wouldn't hear
from her for at least eighteen hours, I made myself wait until the next
morning before my chores, to call her. It had been thirty-six hours, so I
figured she had to be back by now.

I leaned against the store's coffee counter and tried calling the
warden's cell phone, while Packrat made us each a large, three-packet
hot cocoa. Not reaching her there, I tried her office.

Warden Penny answered. "Cooper! Good to hear from you. How
was your campout in the winter fort?"

"Awesome! Thanks for putting in a good word with Mom." I told
her about our recent lynx sighting. She sounded pleased to hear the
kitten was eating.

"It came for your fish! It must be hungry."

"We haven't seen it catch anything on its own," I told her. "So we
left another trout there before heading home."

"Hmm . . . By the way, I've been asking around to see if anyone has
heard about or seen someone with a collared lynx. I haven't had much

luck, though. It's still a mystery. We'll have to talk to Warden Kate if it doesn't start hunting on its own soon."

"That's why I'm calling—to talk to her."

"She isn't back yet. She's probably still out of range. Give her a little longer. This happens all the time—I'm sure you'll hear soon."

Not back yet?

My head hurt with all my questions and what-ifs. Why wasn't she back? Had she found new evidence? Did she find the poacher's camp? What if the person buying the pelts showed up, too?

I started to ask Warden Penny some of these questions, but she cut me off.

"Cooper, I'm sorry, I've got to go. Without Kate, I've got twice the calls to respond to. But keep me in the loop."

I hung up with a sigh.

Packrat looked sympathetic.

"Hopefully, we'll hear from Warden Kate today," I said. "We only have tomorrow and Friday to hike to the crash site."

"She'll call," Packrat assured me.

Roy joined us to help with our morning jobs, and once we'd finished, we were free to do whatever we wanted for the rest of the day.

As we left the store porch, Roy asked, "What should we do? Ice-fishing? Sliding? We haven't—"

"Dogsledding!" Packrat and I reminded him at the same time. There's no way Roy could have forgotten it was on the schedule for today.

I was beginning to think it wasn't the dogsledding he was avoiding.

Packrat and I headed for Wynter's campsite to help her get ready. We dragged Roy along for two reasons. One, we figured we owed her, since she'd talked her mom into giving rides to our customers. And two,

Packrat and I were hoping to finally get on a sled. I thought Roy would like it, too, if he'd just quit being stubborn.

The dogs perked up and danced in place as we stepped onto Wynter's campsite. Summer looked up from filling water pails, and I noticed that even though her eyes met mine, she didn't smile. My heart sank a little.

"Hey," I said, testing to see just how upset at me she was.

"Hey," she replied. Okay, at least she was talking to me.

Wynter stepped out of her camper, slipping on her gloves. "Hey!" she called over to us.

"Hey," Packrat replied.

"Great conversation," Roy muttered.

"Want to help hook the dogs up to the sled?" Wynter asked Roy.

He shrugged. " 'Kay."

Wynter walked to the front of the sled. Her dogs froze in their spots, eyes only on her. As she picked up a long rope from the ground which attached to the front of the sled, the dogs erupted in barking and tail wagging and jumping. Even Raven. Every dog wore a smile!

"You'd think they'd just won the lottery," I said.

Wynter looked fondly at the pack. "They live to pull. But they know they can't all go. Whoever is chosen 'wins.' "

Walking straight out from the sled until the rope was tight, she handed it to Roy.

"This is the gangline. Hold it here while we attach the lead dogs."

She ran to the back of the sled and picked up another rope which was attached there.

"I've got to tie off this snub line. Sometimes they get so excited, they take off before I'm on the sled," she explained, wrapping the rope around the nearest tree trunk. "They don't listen to 'whoa' so well when they're excited."

With the sled secure, Wynter then race-walked to where the dogs were tied to their stakes. For the first time, I noticed Wynter's Chinooks wore bright blue harnesses, which crisscrossed over their backs and down around their chests and bellies.

Unhooking Bear from his tether, she asked me to get Raven.

"With six dogs, we can carry seven hundred pounds on the sled, including me," Wynter said. "That's about two adults and one child."

"Hey, girl." I put my hand on the top of Raven's head, but she didn't even glance my way. Pulling her tether as tight as it would go, and leaning past me, she followed Wynter with her eyes. Raven knew who decided if she could go or not!

"No time for petting," Wynter said while racing past me to the dogsled with Bear. "We have to hook them up fast, so they don't get tangled or rough with each other."

I grabbed hold of Raven's harness and unclipped her tether. Instantly, she took off, almost tugging me off my feet! Half-dragging, half-pulling, Raven led me to the front right side of the rope Roy held. Turning on a dime, she stood next to Bear, facing forward, dancing in place, putting the gangline between them.

I chuckled. "You know your spot, don't you? Lead dog. Impressive."

Wynter smiled my way as she attached a long line to the top of Bear's harness, then attached the other end of it to the gangline behind her dog. I copied the steps, doing the same for Raven, and it earned me another smile.

"Those are tug lines," Wynter explained.

She then hooked Bear and Raven together at their collars with another line. "This is a neckline."

"Makes sense!" Packrat said, taking a few photos. "I can't wait to show everyone at school!"

"You can let go of the rope now," Wynter told Roy. "Bear and Raven will automatically pull, so it will stay tight while we connect the rest of the team."

Summer came over with Grizzly, Packrat brought Fox, and I took Wolf. The only dog remaining was Moose, so Roy went to fetch him.

Wynter put Grizzly and Fox behind Bear and Raven. They had tug lines to attach, too, but they also had shorter lines from their collars to the gangline.

"The neckline helps them stay in formation," Wynter explained. Reaching for Wolf, she added, "Every dog has a position they're best at."

Wynter clipped Wolf's neckline, while I attached the tug line.

"Okay," Wynter said, taking a few steps back, checking every dog. "Wait, where's Moose?"

I shrugged. "Roy went—"

"Crazy dog!"

We turned to find Roy, sprawled on his back in the snow, a snowball still in his hand over his head. Moose sat on his chest, gazing down into Roy's eyes.

Wynter put her hands on her hips. "Moose! This is no time to be playing with Roy! Get over here!" Moose licked Roy's face before bounding over to Wynter.

"Geez! He didn't have to tackle me. I woulda tossed him the snowball," Roy muttered as he took Packrat's hand to get pulled up. Before ducking his head to brush snow off his pants, I caught a glimpse of a smile.

"Mom's coming for you," Wynter called back to the dogs left behind. They were still barking and jumping in a pleeeease-take-me-too kind of way, but without the same level of excitement.

The camper door opened, and Lisa stepped out. Seeing all of us, she gave a quick nod. I gulped, almost afraid to ask, but I knew it was the right thing to do.

"Do you need help hitching up your dogs?"

"They cut my time in half," Wynter said, giving us all a thank-you smile.

"No," Lisa said. "I'm waiting to talk to someone first. You should go. No sense keeping your dogs waiting."

She was right. Wynter's team wiggled and jiggled in anticipation. They barked at us to hurry up but stayed in their positions.

As Wynter double-checked everything, I glanced at Lisa. She stood in the middle of her team now, talking to each one. Her phone rang, and she reached into her coat pocket. As she pulled the phone out, the bottom of her jacket flapped open.

And there, tucked in a holster at her side, was a gun.

I quickly glanced around. No one else had seen it!

"Hello?" Lisa adjusted her coat over the gun as she talked into her phone. "I've been waiting. Let's talk."

CHAPTER 20

Lynx kittens are helpless at birth, but are born with a lot of fur to keep them warm.

I looked everywhere but at Lisa, so she wouldn't guess what'd I'd seen under her coat. Moving closer to Packrat and Roy, I opened my mouth to whisper to them.

"We're ready!" Wynter interrupted me. She jumped on the back of the sled, both feet on the runners, her hands on the handle. There was no time to tell Packrat and Roy.

"Someone can ride in the basket," Wynter offered. "There's room for another on the back with me."

Summer shook her head. "I've had a ride. You guys go."

Wynter looked to Roy.

"I'll walk down with her." My stubborn friend pointed his thumb toward Summer.

"Don't be scared," Wynter said. Seeing Roy stiffen, I cringed inside. No guy likes to be accused of being scared. "The sled goes wicked fast sometimes, but you ride snowmobiles. You can handle it."

"I'm not scared." Roy practically choked out that last word. "I just know Cooper and Packrat are dying to go."

I so badly wanted to tell Roy and Packrat what I'd seen under Lisa's coat, but Summer and Wynter would think it was weird if none of us got on the sled.

"I'll ride on the back," I offered.

"I'll take the basket," Packrat said, stepping inside and pulling out his camera. "I've been dying to get a dog's-eye view of the ride!"

Summer and Roy started walking down the road toward the lake as Packrat settled into the basket.

Wynter pointed to the left runner behind the handle. "You stand on that one, Cooper; I'll take the right." Reaching for the rope tied to the tree behind the sled, she explained, "When I tug this rope, the knot will come undone, and the team is just gonna go. Hold on!"

The dogs were loudly barking and pulling and so excited, I couldn't help but pick up on their energy, too. Packrat shot us a smile over his shoulder, his camera ready to video.

Wynter tugged the rope. We were off!

It got quiet instantly as the dogs pulled us along a snowmobile trail through the woods. They moved fast, too! Without all the barking, you could hear the soft swishing of the runners in the snow. I looked to Raven and Bear. Their tongues were hanging out, their faces beaming.

Turning a corner, we started heading downhill on a straightaway and the dogs really took off! The runners made a whooshing sound now as they cruised through the newly fallen snow on the packed trail. The cold breeze hitting my cheeks held snowflakes kicked up from the dogs' feet.

"I can give rides for about three hours, then I should rest the dogs for a bit and give them water, so they don't get dehydrated," Wynter said.

"We don't have many campers," I said. "You should have plenty of time."

As we rounded the last corner and arrived at the beach area, I saw at least thirty people standing around the campfire while a couple more campers unloaded wood from their trucks and stacked it nearby. Wynter slowed the dogs as we passed fifteen to twenty more who parted for us to slide by, waving and exclaiming how excited they were for their turn.

"On by!" Wynter called to the dogs, while smiling and nodding at the gathering people. "On by!"

I could tell she was proud of what she did. And she should be. It was wicked cool!

Slowing the dogs even more, Wynter called out to everyone waiting, "I'll be right back!"

"You're not stopping?" I asked. Packrat looked back to hear her answer, too.

"Can you show me a good route to take? Maybe a mile one way to give a nice ride? With something interesting to look at?"

"The suspension bridge!" Packrat and I said at the same time.

The sled cruised out onto the snow-covered ice. "Head to the right, toward the end of the lake," I told her.

Wynter's left foot stood on the runner, and she pushed the ground with her right every so often, kind of like you do when riding a skateboard.

"Mom will be down with her team by the time we get back. Dogsledding is popular no matter where we go. Everyone wants to try it. We've been to Pennsylvania, to Maine, and everywhere in between. But Canada, at home, is still my favorite place to take out my team."

"When do you head back?" I asked.

Packrat turned his camera around to catch footage of Wynter driving.

"From here, we're stopping at a town just across the Canadian border for a couple days. Mom has an . . . an appointment—a job. Then we head north toward home. I can't wait." She gave a wistful sigh. "No offense," she added. "It's pretty here, too."

"None taken," I replied. "There's no place like home."

Her home was Canada. Just over the border. An appointment.

The gun in Lisa's holster flashed through my mind.

According to Warden Kate, poacher Thomas Scott sells his illegal furs to someone who takes them over the border to resell them, so they can't be traced back to him.

I sighed. Roy was gonna say "I told you so."

CHAPTER 21

Lynx have long hind legs and can jump twenty-five feet from a crouched position. An average person can jump three feet.

We traveled along smoothly, fifty feet from the right shoreline. This end of the lake was all woods. Bare limbs of birch, maple, and oak mixed with the greens of white pine and hemlock.

"The dogs look like they could go forever!" Packrat called from his seat in the dogsled.

"Have I told you how much they love to pull?" Wynter pushed with her right foot a few times. "Whenever my mom and I have a fight, or I'm sad, I take the dogs out. It's so peaceful. It lets me think."

"I know 'whoa' is stop," I said, "but are there other commands?"

"I use 'whoa,' but it doesn't always work until they're tired enough to hear me." Wynter put both feet on the runner and with her left toe, she touched a rectangular black flap between the runners. "I have a brake."

Of course—there's a brake!

Up ahead, about twenty feet off the right shoreline, a huge boulder was sticking up out of the ice. We'd named it Jumping Rock, because in the summer, we liked to kayak over and cannonball off it.

"Haw! Haw!" Wynter yelled. As one unit, the dogs turned left to put some distance between us and the rock.

"Cool!" I exclaimed. I wasn't sure if it was the cold air, or my comment, but I thought Wynter's cheeks turned a little pinker than usual.

"I use 'gee' for right, 'let's go' for taking off, and 'on by' if they get distracted by a person or animal on the trail. 'Straight ahead' means to go through an intersection. And sometimes," Wynter chuckled, "I say 'Want a cookie?' to get them to go home faster. It's the treat they get when we're all done for the day."

Ten minutes later we'd reached the place I wanted to show Wynter. In the back corner of the lake, a rocky river narrowed before flowing over a man-made rock dam. Behind that, through the bare trees, you could see an old suspension bridge made of cables, rope, and wood over the river.

I pointed to a break in the trees on the right shoreline. "If you wanted a longer ride, you'd get off the ice over there. It connects to the all-purpose trails on Piehl Mountain."

Wynter gently put her foot on the brake to slow the dogs. Panting heavily, they slowed, and slowed, and slowed, before stopping completely. I thought they'd flop to the ground in exhaustion, but instead they whined and barked and danced in place.

The bridge was old. Two cables ran the length of each side, one at the top and one at the bottom. Either end attached to five-foot-tall pillars made of rock and cement. Between the top and bottom cable on each side, thick ropes crossed each other and knotted to the cables to make a bunch of V shapes for sides. More ropes between the bottom two cables helped keep the wooden floor slats in place. Well, what was left of the slats, anyway. My friends and I knew the bridge had been blocked off on each end with CAUTION, NO TRESPASSING, and USE AT YOUR OWN RISK signs.

"The bridge used to be part of an old cart road through town," I told Wynter. "Back then it was the only way to cross the river, so it was used a lot. Our historical society has photos of people crossing with horses and buggies. When the bridge got old and rickety in the 1930s, they put a new tarred road through town to a bigger metal bridge upriver instead of fixing up or tearing down this one. Eventually, the cart road was forgotten and got swallowed up by the woods." I couldn't even tell where the road began or where it ended, and trust me, Packrat, Roy, and I had looked.

"Sometimes we kayak out here to fish in the river. My mom makes me promise to steer clear of the bridge, though. She calls it an attractive nuisance, something that makes people want to see it or use it, in spite of how dangerous it is.

"This is as close as you should get," I explained to Wynter. "See how all the snowmobile tracks turn around here? The ice gets really thin past this point." I pointed to a rock standing twenty feet high on the left shoreline. "This will make an interesting place to take the campers. You can tell them the cart road story."

Wynter smiled. "It's perfect, thanks!" Pulling the brake up, Wynter called, "Let's go!" As the dogs picked up speed, she added, "Haw, haw!" Leaning into the turn, Wynter had the dogs take us back the way we'd come.

I still stood on the left runner, feeling balanced now, enjoying the ride. I could get used to this kind of traveling.

Halfway back, we saw Wynter's mom leaving the camp lakefront with her own team, heading our way.

"Should we stop and explain where to go?" I asked, even though I didn't really want to meet up with Wynter's mom. I hadn't forgotten about the gun, and I kept wondering why she had it. For protection from wildlife? Lots of people who camped in the wilderness carried them. Or was there more to it?

"She'll see my tracks. She'll know."

Suddenly, the roar of a snowmobile came from behind us. Before I could turn to look, the yellow snowmobile flew by on our right! I worried it would spook the dogs, but they only glanced at it.

Today, it was towing a good-sized sled, totally covered with a green tarp. Fishing gear?

The driver still wore the black helmet with the tinted shield, making it impossible to see a face. Whoever it was, when he or she reached Lisa, they slowed and raised a hand.

Lisa raised her hand in response.

I saw Packrat's back stiffen. I knew he was thinking what I was thinking. Had it been a friendly wave? If so, why not wave at us, too?

Or was it an I-know-you wave?

Or a we-need-to-talk wave?

The snowmobiler zoomed away.

I glanced at Wynter. If she knew the driver, she didn't blink.

Lisa approached, and Wynter nodded as they passed. I thought it odd they didn't even smile at each other.

"So," Wynter said, clearing her throat. "My mom, you know, she can be kind of intense. Sorry about what she said to you the other day."

I shrugged, even though it still bugged me. "She was worried about you."

"That's not all." Wynter looked straight ahead. "It's, well . . . she's complicated. She meant what she said. She knows a ton about wilderness stuff, survival stuff, but she never talks to me about her . . . her work, anymore. Or listens to my ideas. It's kind of like what your mom said about the suspension bridge and the attractive nuisance stuff. She's afraid to put ideas in my head."

Wynter turned to look at me.

"I thought all families were like ours. But at that first campfire with you, when Warden Kate and your mom asked you questions about wildlife, and they really, really listened to your answers and opinions? That's what I want from my mom! Maybe it's too late to ask. I don't know. And then . . ."

Packrat looked back over his shoulder with a raised eyebrow.

"Well," Wynter said, "my mom has been more closed off than ever on this trip."

Packrat and I nodded in sympathy. I couldn't help but wonder though . . . is her mom closed off because she has something to hide?

Wynter slowed the dogs a bit as she reached our beach area. Taking a wide loop, she circled around to get them into position to go back out. Once the dogs stopped, she took a curved metal piece from a bag attached to her sled. It looked like two metal J's attached together.

Jamming it into the snow beside her, she kicked it with her heel.

"This is my snow hook," she explained. "There's no tree here to tie the sled to, so this is the next best thing."

Wynter, Packrat, and I surveyed the crowd that had formed while we were on the lake. Starting at an orange cone on the beach area, a line of people waited their turn. Summer was signing people up and giving information. Kids ran everywhere, rolling in the snow and sliding on the ice. Other adults stood around the blazing fire Roy was now tending, sipping hot drinks and chatting.

"Wow! I'm glad we got our ride first!" Packrat exclaimed.

"Me too!" I agreed. "See you after?" I asked Wynter, as I stepped off the sled.

"Sure!" Wynter put a gloved hand to her forehead, shielding her eyes from the sun while scanning the crowd. "I should be done by the time the snow melts."

I was almost afraid she might be right.

Looking around, I suddenly wished Mom and Molly felt better so they could see this. Molly especially. She would have loved a ride on the dogsled with Wynter. Our second Wilder Campground Winter Festival activity was a hit! Dad would be so proud. Hey, maybe I could convince him to make it an annual event! Molly could get her ride next year!

Summer caught my eye, and I gave her a thumbs-up to get started. Cupping a hand around her mouth, she hollered, "Sanchez, party of three!" Checking her list, she added, "Holt, party of two—you're up next!" Summer checked off the names, then added, "Bogdanovitch and Lavallee, stay close by. You're on deck."

I saw the family with the little boy who'd hugged his fish. And the guy who'd taken first place in our derby. Karl had come too, talking to—

Wait! I knew that guy! Grabbing Packrat's coat sleeve, I hissed in his ear. "The poacher!"

"But . . . but . . . what's he doing here?" Packrat looked around wildly. I knew the minute my friend spotted the guy because his whole body stiffened up.

The poacher slipped away from the crowd, edging toward our hiking trail which wound along the edge of the lake, away from the beach area. He pulled his hat with the flaps low over his eyes and put his hands in his pockets.

He'd talked to Karl. It'd been quick. Sure. Maybe they'd just had a Hey-where's-the-bathroom kind of talk. I didn't see him even look at anyone else, but how long had he been here? What was he doing? Why had he come back to the scene of the crime? Could he even do that?

Were they working together?

My radio crackled. "Cooper? You there?"

"I'm at the lake, Mom."

"Karl stopped by the store earlier. Could you deliver wood to his campsite? I've got a case of water jugs for him too. Put them inside his camper, so they don't freeze."

Packrat and I exchanged a glance. "Absolutely, Mom. I'd be happy to."

Dropping the wood loudly at Karl's campsite by his fire ring, I called out, "Hey! Anyone home?"

Packrat jumped off the golf cart. Picking up the case of water from the seat, he carried it over to the camper door. We scanned the area, and not seeing anyone, I knocked hard. "Hello?" I asked one more time, just in case Karl had left the lake and beat us back to his camper.

I put my hand on the door handle and turned. It was locked. I glanced at Packrat. He nodded.

Mom had given me the key and permission to go in after talking to Karl. It was our rental, after all. Why did I feel so jumpy doing it?

Unlocking the door, I stepped inside. Packrat followed, putting the case of water on the dinette table right next to a stack of Karl's brochures. I looked around. I didn't plan to, you know, go through his drawers or anything. Honestly, I hoped we wouldn't find anything suspicious. I liked the guy! He taught kids about nature and exploring the outdoors. Unlike Wynter's mom, he talked to me. He asked me questions, honestly interested in my wildlife stories.

We stood in the main part of his camper, a combination living room, dining room, and kitchen area. On our right hung a curtain covering the doorway to Karl's bedroom. On the left end of the camper was a bathroom.

And there, through a crack in the open bathroom door, I saw a hint of white camouflage in the mirror over the sink. I groaned as I walked the length of the camper. Throwing open the bathroom door, I showed Packrat the one-piece camouflage suit hanging on the back of it.

Packrat turned to leave, shaking his head sadly. I closed the bathroom door. Karl would know I'd been in the camper, but he wouldn't know I'd seen the suit. As I walked by his table, my hand brushed the pile of brochures and they scattered to the floor. I bent to pick them up and put them back. Something in the back of my mind tugged at my memory.

"Cooper?" Packrat called.

I folded the brochure and tucked it in my pocket as I hurried outside to find Packrat crouched down, looking under the camper. His worried eyes met mine.

Two things jumped out at me as I looked to where he pointed. One: The missing snow blind, folded up flat, was lying on the ground behind the camper steps. And two: It smelled an awful lot like fish for a guy who claimed his were stolen.

Suddenly, the pieces smashed together in my brain like two bull moose crashing their racks together in a fight.

"It's Karl! He wants this lynx kitten to be his next mascot! He can't get it, so I bet he's hired that poacher to help him!"

CHAPTER 22

*Lynx have twenty muscles in their ears, which allow
them to move in a half-circle. Listening in many
directions is an important hunting tool. Lynx can hear a
rabbit's foot move or a mouse squeak.*

After the dogsled rides were over, Packrat, Roy, and I left the campfire
burning on the beach so everyone could hang out while Wynter,
Summer, and Lisa took the dogs back to their campsite for a well-
deserved supper and a rest. It was after dark before all the campers
finally meandered back to their sites. We put out the fire, cleaned up,
and crashed in our snow fort, sleeping until the sun rose over the trees.

Packrat, Roy, and I worked for Mom all morning, shoveling last
night's light snow off the porches and then cleaning bathrooms. After
that, we snowshoed the camp's hiking trail looking for signs of the lynx.
The whole time, we compared notes on the clues we'd found so far.
Then we talked about Warden Kate. Why hadn't we heard from her? It
didn't help that Warden Penny wasn't returning my calls, either.

Packrat, Roy, and I had just bitten into our second hamburgers
when Summer walked out of the six o'clock darkness and onto our
campsite to sit across the fire from us. We hadn't seen her or Wynter
all day, although I knew they'd slept in their fort too, because I'd heard
them talking this morning..

"All I'm saying," Packrat said, pointing his burger at Roy, "is if you
eat another huge helping of baked beans, you're banned from our fort
tonight."

Roy snorted. Scooping out the rest of the beans onto his paper plate, he then took his time scraping the sides of the pot over and over to get every last bean and drop of sauce. He shot Packrat a so-there look.

Packrat groaned and clutched his nose. "We'll be dead by morning! Promise me, Summer, you'll tell my mom I love her!"

Laughing out loud, I looked to Summer, expecting her to join in with a snort-laugh. But her face only held a hint of a smile which didn't reach her eyes.

"What's eating you?" Roy said. He was so blunt sometimes! Dipping the end of his roll and burger into his beans, he took a big bite and talked with his mouth full. "You have a fight with what's-her-name?"

"Wynter." Summer stared at him pointedly, "Her name is Wynter, and you know it." One side of her mouth tilted upward. "It's her middle name you don't know."

Roy took another bite and grunted. She had him there.

Summer shifted in her seat and sighed. "So, I went over to Wynter's site just now to see if I could help put the dogs to bed tonight. And . . ." She paused. "If I tell you guys this, you have to promise you won't get all weird about it, okay? It's just something I overheard. It probably doesn't mean anything at all! I only—"

I cut her off gently. "Just tell us what you know, and we'll tell you what we know."

Summer twisted her mittens in her bare hands nervously.

"I was almost to their campsite when Wynter and her mom started arguing. She kept begging her mom to let her do something, or say something. I couldn't quite hear it. But her mom, she got really mad. Told her it was 'none of their business,' that there was more to it that

Wynter didn't know. Then Lisa said . . ." Summer hesitated. "She said if we found out, there was no going back."

"What's that even mean?" Packrat cried.

"It means," Roy spat out, "they're the poachers! Or the fur buyers."

I nodded sadly. "Well, suspects, anyway."

Summer jumped up and began pacing. "Okay. Fine. I'll agree Lisa is! Not Wynter, though. I won't believe it."

"Lisa isn't the only suspect." I took a deep breath. "I think it's Karl. He's after the lynx, but he wants it alive so it can be his new mascot."

Packrat and I told Summer how Karl had talked to the poacher, that he had camouflage gear, and how the outside of the camper reeked of fish.

Summer's expression grew hopeful. "So, I misunderstood! It's Karl we should be watching. Not—"

"Hey!" Wynter walked out of the dark to sit in the empty chair between Roy and me. Settling in, she yawned behind her hand.

How much had she heard? Packrat, Summer, and I shared guilty looks. Roy just leveled her with one of his stares. Anyone else would have squirmed, but Wynter flashed him a smile.

"Hey, Roy!"

Packrat slid his empty paper plate into the fire. In seconds, the flames flickered up to nibble away at it. "Boy, your dogs can pull!" he told her. "No matter how many times they went out yesterday, they always came back and hollered to go again."

"They loved it as much as the riders did," Wynter replied.

"It's a lot of work, though," said Summer.

"It is, but these are my favorite kind of days. The only thing I like better is when Mom and I take the dogs into the middle of nowhere to winter wilderness camp. The stars are bright and twinkly without all the light pollution. Twice, I saw the aurora borealis!" Wynter looked to Summer. "Mom says we can take you sometime."

Summer played with her mittens, and I saw her biting her bottom lip. I knew she felt guilty for telling us what she'd heard.

Leaning forward in my chair, I held my hands over the blazing, crackling hot flames in the fire ring.

I'd run a quick plan by Packrat and Roy today while snowshoeing. Packrat had agreed. Roy wanted in, but not with the girls. I'd insisted we needed them. Wynter was key, and no way was I leaving Summer out of our adventure. It wouldn't be as much fun.

I wasn't surprised Packrat had backed me up. I'd bet anything he wanted to spend more time with Summer. And her with him.

After Summer's report on Wynter and Lisa, I looked to Packrat and Roy with a silent question: *Still in?*

Go for it was their silent message back.

"So, we've got trouble," I began. Summer and Wynter leaned in.

"What kind of trouble?" Wynter asked.

"We saw the poacher after our dogsled run."

"What?" Wynter cried.

"Here?" Summer groaned.

I watched Wynter for a sign—any sign—that she knew the guy, or knew he'd been here, at least. But she seemed as surprised as we were. Summer and Wynter started talking over each other.

"You should call Warden Penny!"

"What about Warden Kate?"

"Whoa!" I stood and held up my hands to make them stop so I could answer. "Warden Kate's phone is still out of range. Warden Penny hasn't returned my calls since Tuesday." I tapped the fire ring with the toe of my boot in frustration. "I'm not surprised by Warden Penny. She's nice and all, but you know how some adults are. If she were here, she'd pinch my cheek, pat me on the head, and tell me not to worry."

"My mom does that," Wynter grumbled. "I hate it."

"Me, too." Summer nodded.

"Me, three," Packrat chimed in.

We all looked to Roy. His eyebrows went down. "What? Nobody better pinch my cheek or talk to me like a five-year-old."

I chuckled. "Roy, trust me, no one would ever pat you on the head for fear of getting bit."

"Got that right."

Grabbing another log, I threw it on the fire. "My gut tells me Warden Kate is in trouble." Everyone looked at me expectantly.

I lowered my voice. "Warden Kate asked us to stay in the campground for a few days while she went to investigate the poacher's camp." I stopped short of telling the girls the part about the poacher selling off illegal pelts in a hurry, just in case Wynter's mom turned out to be the buyer. "She told me she'd call in eighteen hours, but it's been three days! What if she ran into him? What if he has a partner? What if they've got her and won't let her go? Wardens take a lot of risks when they track down poachers alone!"

Roy, lounging in his chair, studied Wynter.

"The crash site is a whole day's hike from here, one way." I didn't sugarcoat the facts. "But . . ."

"If we took the dogs," Wynter said softly, "we could be there and back in a day."

Yes! That's what I was hoping for!

"You'd do that?" I asked.

Wynter shrugged. "Sure. I mean, I think so."

"Wait a minute!" Roy pointed a finger at her. "Which is it—you can or you can't? Don't mess with Cooper's hopes! I bet your mom wouldn't let you go that far on your own. And she wouldn't let you take us." He turned to me. "We'll take my snowmobile."

Wynter pointed back at him. "My mom is leaving before dawn tomorrow to . . . to get supplies for our ride home. She said she'd be gone all day, so she doesn't have to know. Besides, dogsledding is quieter, and we're on a rescue mission."

"Snowmobiles are faster!"

"No, they're actually—"

"Cocoa anyone?" Packrat opened the left side of his jacket, slid a hand in an inner pocket, and pulled out a handful of packets. We all mumbled yes as the two hotheads slumped back into their seats and crossed their arms.

"We've only got three days of February vacation left," Summer warned. "Tomorrow, then the festival on Saturday, and Roy, Packrat, and Wynter go home Sunday."

"I know," I told her. Quietly I said, "That's why it's got to be tomorrow."

I'm in," Roy growled. He was done planning. He just wanted to go.

"I'm in," Packrat said.

"Me, too," Summer agreed.

"Wouldn't miss it," Wynter said solemnly.

CHAPTER 23

Lynx have a hyoid bone, a horseshoe-shaped bone that sits in the front of the neck, which allows them to purr loudly, but not roar.

As we drank the cocoa, we checked the weather on three different apps. Tomorrow would start out sunny, but snow squalls—quick, fast snowstorms—were kinda-sorta predicted for about five o'clock. I wanted to be home and not playing a game of nighttime manhunt by then.

The best news, though, was that the snowmobile trail from the end of our lake all the way to the Hercules crash site had been reported groomed and open.

"It's about sixty miles one way." I took a deep breath, then let my timeline thoughts loose. "We can travel fifteen to twenty miles an hour; we'll need to stop to rest ourselves and the dogs a couple of times, with water and snacks; find Warden Kate, talk to her for an hour; check to be sure the poacher doesn't have the lynx; then turn around to be home for suppertime. So, we need to leave at six-thirty tomorrow morning." I stood in the middle of my circle of friends, looking for nods or questioning faces. But everyone had turned to Packrat.

"Hey!" he cried, eyes wide. "Why is everyone staring at me?"

"Because," Roy said, "you can't wake up before nine o'clock unless a coyote howls right next to your ear and there's hot cocoa under your nose!"

"I can so—for important stuff!" Packrat insisted. "And this is important."

"It's not only Warden Kate we're worried about," I explained. "The lynx didn't eat the other fish we left for it. We haven't heard it call in two nights, and there weren't any signs in last night's snow when we snowshoed today."

Summer moaned. "We looked too and came up empty. We hoped you'd seen some."

"Maybe it moved on with the adult?" Wynter suggested.

"Yeah, right," Roy scoffed. "You'd want us to think that. Maybe it met up with a unicorn who took it to a magical land—"

"Ahem!" I interrupted, glaring at Roy. "The poacher visited here yesterday late morning. There's a wicked good chance he grabbed it, after trapping it the night before. Maybe lured it in with food. We can't waste any time."

I pulled a list from my pocket.

"We'll all pack our own sandwiches, make it two or three, just in case we're out longer than we plan. Add some snacks. An extra layer of clothes. First-aid kit. Extra blankets."

"Wood," Roy said. "Just some small stuff in case we need to make a fire." I added it to my list, along with a fire starter and matches. "I'll tow a sled behind my snowmobile to help carry supplies so someone can sit behind me."

"I have to bring food for the dogs, and straw for them to lie down in." Wynter told us. "They can't lie in the snow." I started to write it down, but she shook her head. "I have everything I need, and the dogs' emergency aid kit is always ready to go. Mom's leaving about six in the morning, and Summer and I had planned to hang out and go dogsledding all day anyway." Wynter shrugged. "So, I'm ready for a long day on the trail."

Roy raised an eyebrow, and I didn't have to dig deep to figure out why. The poacher was out there somewhere. I hadn't heard from

Warden Kate. The lynx was missing. And Lisa was off from dawn until dark tomorrow, without Wynter?

No. Nothing suspicious there.

"I've got a camera, binoculars, screwdriver, and wrench," Packrat offered, patting a pocket.

"Dad brought home a case of gallon jugs of water. I'll bring a couple," Summer said. "Everyone pack a water bottle and we'll refill."

"Can anyone think of anything else?" I asked.

Four serious faces looked back at me.

"Soooooo," I had to ask one more time, "you're all still okay to go? I mean, it's a long way there and back. I'll be grounded for a week when Mom finds out, and she'll find out eventually. But I can't sit here and do nothing while the lynx kitten and Warden Kate are missing!"

"As long as we do it in a day." Summer had a glint in her eye which told me she couldn't wait to begin. "Dad knows I'm with Wynter."

"Packrat's mom and my mom think we're going over to the Wayside Inn cellar hole. You know," I said to Summer, "the one where we dug up the old bottles and found the bear cub." Summer hadn't been on that adventure with us, but she'd insisted I take her to see it when she got back from visiting her mom. "Besides, now my mom has Molly's cold. The two of them will be on the couch watching movies and dozing on and off all day."

"There is one thing," Wynter said. "It'd help a lot if I could put the straw and dog food in Roy's sled. Then I'd have room for—"

Roy sat up straight. "Wait, wait, wait. I didn't catch that last part. Can you ask me again?" His grin said he'd heard her loud and clear, but he wanted to rub it in.

"Roooooy!" Summer leaned forward, pointing at him the best she could with her mitten on, and giving him a knock-it-off-or-I'm-coming-over-there stare.

Wynter held up a hand. I had to give her credit. She didn't look like she wanted to tell him to shut up or anything. She looked . . . tired.

"Okay, Roy. I'll play it your way for the sake of the mission." She cleared her throat, and very deliberately said, "I need your help."

Roy burst out laughing, rocking back on his butt, before rolling forward again. "I knew you'd need my help to get out on the trail! Snowmobiles rule!"

"Listen, Roy," Wynter drew out his name in annoyance. "It takes a lot of work to—"

"Admit it!" Roy crowed.

Wynter's face turned dark. Packrat and I shot each other a look across the tent.

"Hey!" I warned. "Get serious, Roy! I need you both!"

"Looks like all you need is me!" Roy slapped a knee with his hand.

Wynter stood, then stormed to the tent opening. "You jerk! You've gone too far this time! I didn't have to offer to help! It's a lot of work to get the team ready for a run. I have to cover their feet, feed them early and well, and hook them up. And when we get back, I've got to do it again in reverse! I can't just pour some stupid gas in a tank."

Roy stopped laughing to stare at her. She wasn't finished.

"And . . . and . . . and turn a key to get where we need to go. Your way," she paused for effect, "is the easy way!"

"It's not easy! You're the jerk!" Roy jumped up to point a finger at her. "Wynter Squall!"

Wynter narrowed her eyes and opened her mouth, but Roy threw more words at her. "You're so full of gusty hot air all the time! And by the way, that wasn't a guess, either!"

Summer stood with Wynter. The girls glared at Roy.

"That might not have been a guess," Wynter said quietly, "but you won't get a chance to make your fifth."

The girls stormed off toward their site.

"It's *not* easy!" Roy mumbled when they were out of earshot.

"Compared to what she's got to do, it kind of is." The words tumbled from my mouth before I thought about them. But since I'd said it, I thought I might as well say the rest. "Why do you pick on her all the time? She's right—she doesn't have to help!"

"Don't you guys get it?" Roy stood, towering over us. "She's only coming along so she can keep us out of her mom's hair tomorrow! You said Lisa got an important call right when you noticed her gun. What if she talked to the poacher? Arranged a time to collect the pelts? You two are so dumb sometimes!"

Roy turned on his heel and stormed away into the darkness in the opposite direction of the girls' fort.

CHAPTER 24

Lynx are built for the cold.

At six-thirty the next morning, Packrat and I stood at the edge of the lake in the gray, predawn light, my backpack full of supplies, his coat pockets bulging. We both glanced up the road and sighed.

"How long should we give them?" Packrat asked.

I looked at my cross-country skis. Packrat and I had waffled on whether snowshoes or skis would be better, but we both knew it would take twice as long either way. Packrat had done some quick calculations, and honestly, we didn't think we could get there and back in a day without Wynter's dogs or Roy's snowmobile. If they didn't show, however, we planned to see how far we could get.

I needed my friends to show. All of them.

I looked at my watch. It was 6:32. Two minutes? Sheesh! It felt like two years.

Packrat and I had crawled into our sleeping bags last night, waiting and waiting for Roy to come back. I'd gotten so worried I'd waffled on calling Mom. I wasn't a snitch or anything, but honestly, where else could he sleep overnight? His parents weren't here, he was officially staying with Packrat, and it was only twenty-eight degrees outside.

Around nine, I'd had my finger on my radio button when he'd slid into the tent without a word. Crawling into his sleeping bag, he'd faced the wall.

I'd breathed a sigh of relief, but when my alarm went off at five-thirty the next morning, he'd already gone.

"Is Roy right?" Packrat must have been thinking about him, too. "Is Wynter just keeping us from crossing paths with her mom?"

I shook my head. "My hunch says it's Karl we've got to watch out for. But——"

A loon's tremolo call rang out around us. Packrat whirled to look at the ice-covered lake. "How? Aren't all the loons in the ocean right now?"

I pulled out my phone and waggled it at him. Laughing, he punched me on the arm. "You have the weirdest ringtones!"

"I bet it's Summer or Roy, asking us to wait up!" Seeing the number, though, I frowned. I didn't recognize this one.

Packrat looked over my shoulder. "Hurry up and answer! Maybe it's Wynter!"

Of course! I hit the green button, then the speaker button so Packrat could hear, too. "Hey!" I said, "Where are——"

Static came through. Then nothing.

"I can't hear you!" I wasn't sure why I yelled back; either they had a bad connection or dead air. "Summer? Wynter? Try hanging up and calling ag——"

"Cooper!"

It wasn't Wynter or Summer. Or Roy. It was Warden Kate!

"What's wrong?" I said, as Packrat and I exchanged worried glances. "Are you okay?"

"Cooper! I'm glad I got ahold of you. Listen, I . . ."

Silence.

"Warden Kate? Are you there?"

Packrat signaled me to walk off to the left a little, toward the ice.

"Hello? Hello?" I asked every few steps.

Just as suddenly she returned. "Can you hear me? Oh, come on!"

"I hear you!"

"Thank goodness! Cooper, I know I'm late getting back! I ran into trouble . . ."

Silence again.

"Aaaaaah!" I yelled. I wanted to shake the phone, toss it to the ground, and stomp on it!

"Hello? Hello?" The warden's voice sounded as frustrated as I felt.

"I'm here!" I stood stone still, worried I'd lose her again.

"Cooper, you can't trust . . . I need you to . . ."

Silence.

No, no, no, no! What the heck!

The call disconnected.

"Quick!" Packrat cried as the two of us huddled over the phone. "Get her back!"

We tried. And tried.

No connection.

"What do you think she meant?" he asked.

"Just what she said! She needs us. She ran into trouble!"

Suddenly, the memory of two flashlights in the woods the night the lynx got trapped in the cage came to mind. "The poacher must be working with someone! Why didn't I think of this before? Maybe it's two against one out there. We have to go!"

I looked up the road, then glared at the skis attached to my boots. Suddenly, I envied Roy his snowmobile. It'd take so long to get to her this way!

"Why didn't she call Warden Penny?" Packrat was already clipping his boots to his skis.

"She hasn't been answering my calls, and you heard Warden Kate's connection. But I'll try again."

I put the phone to my ear as I attached my own skis. Warden Penny's phone rang and rang. When her voicemail came on, I left a message.

"Warden Penny? I just got a strange call from Warden Kate. I think she's in trouble." I hesitated. But if I didn't tell her everything and something happened to Warden Kate, it'd be my fault for withholding information. "Packrat and I saw the poacher Wednesday in the campground. I don't think he gave up on catching the lynx. Call me back!"

Swoosh swish. Heavy panting. I knew those sounds!

Packrat and I turned. I almost laughed in relief to see Wynter and a load of gear being pulled by a team of five dogs. Summer jogged behind her with three more on leashes. I looked hopefully behind them, but Roy wasn't there.

Neither Wynter nor Summer was smiling, but they were here. The four of us did this silent, awkward nod thing to each other. I guess it was our way of burying the hatchet until we could really hash things out.

"Warden Kate called," I began.

Summer's face grew worried, and she came a little closer to me with Raven, Wolf, and Fox. "Is she okay?"

My worry over the warden had me forgetting my nervousness around Summer.

"Her call kept breaking up. All I heard was that she's run into trouble, and she needs me. Needs us."

And not to trust someone. Wynter? Lisa? Karl?

Summer and Wynter looked at each other.

"We're in," Summer finally said. "But it's for Warden Kate."

"And the lynx," Wynter added. She looked around. "So, no Roy?"

"No Roy," I said.

Wynter threw her hook into the snow and stepped on it to keep her dogs from moving forward. "I didn't figure him for a quitter."

Digging through the bag on the sled, she took out three long lines, three wide belts, and a pair of skis like Packrat's and mine. Dropping the skis at Summer's feet, she handed the blue belt to me, and the red one to Packrat.

"I thought we might need more than just my dog team, but I didn't dare take too many of Mom's dogs. So I'll make do with five on the sled, and that leaves three for you."

Handing Summer a dark blue belt, she said to us all, "Put these on around your hips, not your waist. Make sure they're tight, but not too tight." Standing before us, with a line in each hand that matched our belts, she smiled her first smile since getting off the sled.

"Are you going to pull us?" Packrat asked.

"Nope." Wynter clipped the blue line to my belt and the red one to Packrat's. "Raven, Fox, and Wolf are."

I couldn't stop the grin from forming on my face. "Skijoring!" I breathed.

Wynter brought Raven to me. As she hooked my line to Raven's harness, I realized the line was more like a bungee cord. Summer got Fox, and looked as if she'd been handed a real fox kit to snuggle.

"Packrat," Wynter said, while checking our gear, "I'll give you Wolf."

Standing up, she grabbed our backpacks and put them in the basket on her sled with the dog's food and straw. Without Roy and his sled, there wasn't any room left for her to carry a passenger. Thank goodness Wynter had thought of a backup plan so we could travel faster too!

Raven sat three feet away, looking at me with a happy smile, tail wagging, tongue hanging out.

I think I wore a goofy happy smile, too.

"I love skijoring," Wynter said. "So, all the dogs know how to do it. But those three," she said, looking fondly at her dogs, "they're the best of the bunch.

"The calls are the same as on the sled." Wynter stood in the middle of us, explaining the gear. " 'Gee' is right. 'Haw' is left. 'On by' is to go past something on the trail, and use 'Hike, hike,' if you want them to pick up the pace."

Putting her hand on the bungee line where it attached to my belt, she unclipped it in one move by squeezing the ends together.

"If your dog takes off after something or it looks like you're about to do a nosedive, or you think the dog might get hurt, unclasp fast. Don't worry, they'll know you've done it and come back to you."

"And what if we need to stop?" Packrat asked.

" 'Whoa' or 'wait' works."

Gee, haw, on by, whoa, hike. I scratched my head, struggling to remember all the calls and what they meant.

"That was a crash course in skijoring, I know." Wynter climbed on the back of her sled. "Don't worry, I'll be calling the same commands. These dogs are so experienced, you won't need to do it often."

Raven pulled as far out as she could go on her lead, looking back at me, eager to run. I glanced up the camp road toward the campground one more time, hoping to hear the roar of Roy's snowmobile. Although how I'd hear him over the happy, excited barking of the dogs, I didn't know.

"Okay?" I asked Packrat and Summer. But I needn't have asked. They looked as excited to start this adventure as I was.

Wynter stood tall on her runner, checking over the dogs pulling her sled. River held the lead position. Behind her, in pairs, were Blizzard and Moose, then Grizzly and Bear. Each of the team looked back at Wynter expectantly, dancing in place.

"You lead," she told me, her hand on the rope to pull her brake from the snow.

Packrat, Summer, and I pulled on our gloves and adjusted our ski poles. I noticed Wynter looked back one more time, too. She shook her head sadly.

"Let's go!" I hollered to Raven, immediately stiffening, waiting for a hard tug forward. It never came. Instead, I slid forward smoothly, easily. Digging into the snow with my poles on either side of me, I pushed myself along while alternating my skis like I'd normally cross-country ski, only I felt myself being half-pulled by Raven at the same time. This was so much faster! It was so much fun! It was—

Suddenly, the ground felt as if it was tilting beneath me. I waved my arms like a newborn duckling and bent my knees, but I couldn't stop my fall. Oooof! I hit the ground, landing hard on my side in the

snow. Raven dragged me a foot or two, before coming back to push my shoulder with her nose. She seemed to say, 'Really? A nap? Now?'

Hearing giggles, I sat up. Summer and Packrat were on the ground, too.

Wynter chuckled. "I was waiting for that. Try again. It takes a minute to feel the rhythm."

Actually, it took fifteen minutes worth of starts and falls to get going. Fifteen minutes of grunts and groans. Fifteen minutes we didn't have! Wynter kept giving us tips and tricks, until finally we were gliding along without wobbling. Mostly.

I looked behind me and saw Packrat concentrating hard, his coat buttoned all the way, the bottom of it flapping open in the breeze. Summer followed, looking everywhere around her, taking it all in. Wynter and her team took the rear.

We headed out onto the ice, taking a right toward the end of the lake with the old suspension bridge. The sun peeked over the trees, brightening the light and welcoming us into our adventure.

Suddenly, a flash of red came up from behind on my right, about twenty feet away.

Roy! He'd made it!

He looked at me through his helmet shield and nodded once. Pointing in front of me, he tilted his head questioningly. I knew he was asking if he should go ahead and check the trail before us.

Smiling, I gave him a thumbs-up, and he zoomed ahead, towing a black, plastic sled filled with his gear behind him.

I sighed in relief. I wasn't sure how long this truce would last between my friends. I didn't know what we'd find out on the trail. Was Roy right? Was Wynter's mother here to buy illegal pelts to take over the border? Had Warden Kate been ambushed by the poacher and an unknown helper? Had Karl caught the lynx?

I had more questions than a duck had ducklings!

Here we come, Warden Kate, I thought. She'd help us sort the rest out. I just hoped we weren't too late.

CHAPTER 25

*Canada lynx need large territories. In Maine, males
tend to claim twenty-two square miles, while females
average ten. They will travel long distances for food.*

We traveled the lake to the inlet where it met the groomed ATV trail
leading into the hundred acres of woods. Shortly after, we turned right
at the fork with the giant boulder, passing the left-hand turn to the
suspension bridge. The trail was just wide enough for two snowmobiles
here. Wynter, Summer, Packrat, and I stayed two by two most of the
time, talking very little as we moved along.

Roy traveled solo well ahead of us.

After an hour, we arrived at a clearing with a gorgeous view in all
directions. We couldn't pull off the trail, as the snow was too deep here.
A snowmobile or sled would sink down into it, and it'd be a bear of a
job to get it back on the trail. Instead, we found a wide spot on the trail,
parking one behind the other on the side to take a quick break.

Ahead in the distance Piehl Mountain rose high. Behind us lay Pine
Lake.

Wynter gave the dogs a drink and spoke to them as Summer,
Packrat and I wearily pulled out a snack and sucked down some water
too. Roy stood alone by his sled, rubbing his head after taking off his
helmet.

I walked over with a bottle of water and an orange. "Everything
good?" I asked, testing his mood.

He nodded, accepting my offer.

"Before we left, I checked the spot where we'd last seen the lynx," said Roy. "No tracks at all in the area. And the fish we left is still there." He took a swig of water. Looking me in the eye for the first time, he said, "I'm worried about the kitten."

I wondered if he'd have come otherwise.

Our second stop at the two-hour mark was much the same. More water, more snacks and more sore muscles. And once again, Roy parked a distance away. I offered to switch places, to let him try skijoring. But he shook his head.

Roy gave me the same answer at the two-and-a-half-hour mark, too. This time, though, he hadn't parked quite so far away. I pretended not to notice when he shifted the dogs food and our backpacks from Wynter's sled to his own plastic sled to lighten their load.

"This next section of trail," Wynter said, "is narrower and goes uphill. But after that, there's a wide-open area with awesome views."

I turned to her. She knew where we were? She must have seen the look on my face because she quickly added, "Mom and I rode through here when we first arrived." Wynter knelt to check Fox's booties and I caught Roy's eye. I steeled myself, expecting a told-you-so grin. Instead, I found a worried Roy. I understood in a flash.

We were almost four hours from home, with no adults, in the middle of nowhere. If Wynter had agreed to help so she could keep an eye on us while her mother bought the pelts, we were on our own now. During the last few years, when we'd tried to save wildlife from bad guys, we'd kinda-sorta gotten into some trouble.

This wasn't going to be one of those times, was it?

We took off again with Roy in the lead, zooming ahead to make sure the trail was clear and groomed. I followed, then Packrat, then Summer, with Wynter still taking up the rear.

Wynter was right; the trail did narrow, probably because of the thick woods we were traveling through. Pines, maples, birches, and oaks stood tall and proud as far as we could see. We'd only come across one other snowmobiler so far today, but still, we kept our eyes peeled.

On an uphill stretch now, our travel speed slowed a bit. I helped Raven as much as I could by using my poles. *We make a good team!* I thought, looking down at her with a grin. She looked back adoringly.

A fork in the trail came into view, and I remembered we needed to go right, based on a map I'd downloaded.

"Gee," I called to Raven. I heard Packrat use it behind me, then Summer, then Wynter. Raven turned to the right, hesitated, and stopped dead in her tracks. I slid to a stop right beside her.

A moose! And not just any moose. A huge bull moose! It stood on the right side of the trail.

Seconds later, Packrat and Wolf joined us. I put up a hand to silently alert Summer.

Wynter—and the dogs! I turned to warn her, but she'd already spied the moose, and was struggling to get the dogs to stop. I stepped into River's path, putting out a hand to grab her harness, slowing the dogs. Wynter's team slid up beside us.

When the dogs saw why we'd stopped, the yipping and barking started in earnest.

The moose's antlers curved inward, looking at least five feet apart. I'd once read that a bull's antlers got bigger and bigger every year. This tells younger bulls, *Don't mess with me, or mine*. This guy? He was carrying his rack a little late in the season. Most moose dropped that weight between November and early March. Carrying them around all the time must be a lot of work!

Maybe that's why this guy looked a little mad?

The moose snorted, twice. It pawed the ground with its hoof, then stomped forward until it stood in the middle of the road, staring us down like a cowboy in a gunfight in an old Western movie.

Roy had stopped beyond the moose by about forty feet. Turned on his seat toward us, he sat still as stone with his machine idling. The moose must have stepped into the trail after Roy had passed.

The moose's ears went back. The hair on its shoulders stood straight up.

Uh-oh. This was bad. Really bad.

Some people think moose are nothing more than gentle cows. That's like saying an eagle is like a mallard! With their long, skinny legs, a moose can run thirty-five miles an hour. Their head is twice the size of ours, and when they decide to rear back to attack with their front hooves, you'd better not be underneath when all their weight comes crashing down.

Looking at the dogs, who were barking at the moose, my heart beat faster. If the moose charged, the dogs could get hurt. Especially the ones attached to Wynter's gangline. There'd be no way for them to escape. No way for us to unhook them all in time.

What should we do? Think! *Think!*

Wynter, moving only her head, looked to me.

I mouthed, *Stay with the sled*.

With no sudden moves, I unclipped the line attached to me, but didn't let it go. I didn't want Raven running out there, trying to protect us or anything. Packrat followed my lead, unclasping Wolf.

"If it's gonna charge, I want it to be at me," I whispered to Packrat. "I don't want it to stomp Wynter's dogs. I'll draw it into the woods. Moose usually give up the fight when they've made their point."

I handed Raven's line to Packrat. I swear that dog shot me a what-the-heck-you-need-me look. "Stay," I told her.

I hit the release for both my skis, stepped out of them, then in front of them.

"I'm hoping those big antlers weigh you down, buddy," I whispered to the moose.

Sidestepping carefully, I eased my way in front of the dog team, then stepped off the trail into the snow on the right.

The moose lowered its head, then raised it up to shake its antlers menacingly my way.

"That's it, big guy," I whispered. "I'm the one you want."

The moose smacked its lips. Uh-oh. A charge sign!

Wynter slid into the middle of her dogs, trying to quiet them.

The moose's eyes locked on mine. It turned toward me. I counted under my breath, "One. Two. Three. Go!"

I took off for the trees. I couldn't be sure at first if the moose had taken me as bait, until I heard hooves pounding and heavy breathing. I swear I felt spit on the back of my neck.

I ran as fast as my feet would go, jumping over fallen trees, pushing branches out of the way, running in a zigzag way to put obstacles between us in hopes he wouldn't hit his max speed.

Seeing a massive boulder, I ducked behind it, leaning against it and closing my eyes. Taking in big gulps of air, I tried to fill my lungs. Running through the snow was hard!

Opening my eyes, I peeked behind the boulder only to find the moose right there! It snorted, backed up, and lowered its antlers.

Suddenly, Raven raced from the thicket to stand between us. Growling low in her throat, tail down, the hair on the back of her neck stood straight up. Raven meant business.

The moose lowered his head and shook his antlers again.

Raven's response was to growl again.

The moose backed up, then backed up some more. It was panting almost as hard as I was.

I whistled softly. Not letting her guard down, Raven backed up until she stood beside me, her eyes staying on the moose until, eventually, it snorted again and then took a wide path around us. I saw its shoulders roll— shoulders higher than my head—its own head and rack looming over me. Pausing, I swear it gave me one last *So there* look from the corner of its eye.

I took a great gulp of air, realizing for the first time I'd been holding my breath. Putting my back against the boulder, I slowly slid down until my butt hit the ground.

Raven licked my face, then trotted toward the trail. Stopping, she looked back and gave two shakes of her tail in a that-was-fun way.

"Thanks, girl!" I said as I stood on shaky legs. "You did good."

CHAPTER 26

In Maine, lynx have been protected from hunting and trapping since 1967.

When I stepped from the woods with Raven, Summer raced forward. We almost fell in a heap in the snow when she threw her arms around my neck and hung on. "We were so worried!" she cried.

Roy snorted. "You were worried. The rest of us knew he'd be fine."

Summer let me go, put her hands on her hips, and stared him down.

"Okay, okay," he admitted. "I might have made a little bit of noise about going after you in five minutes."

"Raven took me by surprise and pulled me off my feet," Packrat explained. He had his bomber hat in one hand and his other on top of his head. "She's okay, right? No way she was letting you tackle the moose on your own, I guess."

Wynter gave me a quick, little hug. "Thanks," she said simply.

"No big deal!" Roy said, narrowing his eyes in a warning kind of way. "Cooper just did what he always does. He reads the wildlife situation and saves the day." He put on his helmet and walked backward. "Let's go!"

Packrat, Summer, and I exchanged looks. What was that all about?

I worried that dealing with the moose had cost us forty-five minutes of daylight. But we took a quick vote and decided to keep going.

After another forty minutes or so of traveling uphill, we finally got to level land. The woods trail opened up to a clearing. The trees around its edges were shorter, and I realized we'd arrived at the peak of Piehl

Mountain. The views were gorgeous! We could see mountains and lakes in the distance. Houses looked no more than a quarter-inch tall.

The gray puffy clouds in the distance, though, had me a little worried.

Loon calls rang out. Raven looked over her shoulder at me, but she was the only one who'd heard my phone.

"Whoa!" I called.

Raven kept going.

"Whoa!"

I swear she was ignoring me! I gently pulled on the tether between us, and hollered again, "WHOOOAAA!"

Raven slowed, but not without looking back with a frowny dog face.

Wynter's team pulled up beside me. Roy's sled had already turned a sharp corner up ahead; there was no way to stop him now.

"What's up?" Summer asked.

I pulled off my right glove with my teeth. Digging into my pants pocket under my ski pants, I pulled out my phone. I glanced at the screen. "Someone's trying to call," I said.

"Who?" Packrat had come back to join us.

I glanced at my recent calls list. "Karl."

"He's got your number?" Wynter asked.

I shrugged. "I gave it to him when he first got here, when he needed wood and water."

"Don't call him," Summer pleaded.

"He might have a question. He's supposed to give his wildlife talk on the trails today."

"If you don't call, he'll go looking for us in the campground," Packrat pointed out.

I groaned. I'd always heard my dad say, darned if you do, darned if you don't.

But I knew two things. One, Packrat was right. If I didn't call, Karl would go looking for me. And two, if he got Mom worried because he couldn't find me, then she'd call. But not me. Oh no. She'd call the US Army and Navy to come find me. The Navy Seals. Maybe all three!

I had to call him back. But we really didn't have the time to spare!

My friends moved in among the dogs to pet and settle them a bit as I put the phone on speaker. Holding the phone out and turning the sound up, I felt my hand shake, I was so nervous.

"Cooper!" Karl's voice, loud and clear.

Darn it! I'd hoped for a bad connection.

"Hey, you called?" I tried to act all cool. Like I was out ice-fishing or something, not traveling a hundred miles to hunt down a lynx stealer and save my game warden or anything.

"Yeah. I wondered . . ." Karl cleared his throat. "Well, first, thanks for the bundles of wood the other day."

"You got them? Good. That's good." I put my free hand on top of my head and looked skyward. Lame!

Packrat swirled his pointer finger in the air, as if to say, *Wrap it up!*

"Okay," I said, nodding to Packrat, "glad to hear it. I've got to go."

"No, wait!" Karl's voice got sharper. "Where are you? I want to thank you personally."

"No. Not necessary. No, uh, worries." My words were rushing together, my panic coming through in my voice. I took calming breaths.

Summer made a breaking motion with her hands.

Breaking. *Breaking?*

She rolled her eyes as Karl began talking. "I could use some, well, advice."

Breaking up! Like what happened during Warden Kate's call.

I made a hissing sound with my voice. "You're break—" I stopped on purpose and looked at Packrat. "Can't hear . . ."

One corner of Packrat's mouth went up. I smiled back.

"Cooper? Cooper? Come on! I need to know where you are!" His voice rose a pitch. I didn't answer right away. Packrat swirled his finger again.

"We're ice-fish . . ."—one, two, three—". . . home soon. No worries."

"Cooper! If you can hear me, I know you went inside my camper! Your boot prints made tracks to my bathroom. You saw my camouflage suit. I wanted to talk to you yesterday about this, but I had my library presentation. If you're trying to get my lynx—"

I hit the hang-up button.

His lynx? *His lynx!*

"I was right!" I told them. "He's trying to get the lynx for a mascot! He thinks it's his! Now we've got to beat him there!"

Summer burst out, "What if he's already on the way, Cooper? He has an ATV! What if he called you from the trail? What if he's up ahead?"

All of Summer's what-ifs had me worried now. What had I gotten us into?

Wynter got back on her sled. "It's another forty minutes or so. Maybe less."

"We'll beat him there," Packrat assured me.

Raven stood, wagging her tail. She knew we were heading out again. "C'mon, girl," I said. "Let's go."

Low roaring sounds filled the field, getting louder and louder by the second. Roy's snowmobile? No, he'd gone on ahead, and these sounds were coming from behind.

Summer grabbed my arm.

"I've got nowhere to go!" Wynter cried, pulling her brake from the snow.

"Off the trail!" I hollered.

We all lifted the sled and moved it off the trail into the knee-deep snow. Wynter ran around to help the dogs so they wouldn't get tangled. I grabbed Raven by her collar, while Summer and Packrat did the same with Wolf and Fox. Just as we got the last dog off the trail, a yellow blur burst up and over the small knoll behind us, leaving the ground for a second. Not slowing at all, it zoomed by without a wave or a glance.

The yellow snowmobile? What the heck was it doing out here? Traveling in the same direction as us?

Wynter yelled a few not-so-nice words.

"Trail hog!" Summer joined in. I felt her shaking beside me. I couldn't blame her. My heart was beating against my ribs, double time.

"C'mon," I put a hand on her arm. "Let's help Wynter lift the sled out."

Packrat waved his phone at me. "When we get back," he threatened, "I'm gonna send a picture and report that crazy snowmobiler once and for all."

"Yes!" I cried. "Brilliant!" Something told me though, that the snowmobiler might be more than just a 'crazy driver.'

Once we were moving forward again, the sights and sounds around me took hold. My heart slowed from our near miss with the snowmobile. My breathing returned to normal. The sun shone brightly down on my shoulders. The trail was smooth and Raven was a great puller, never jerking me off my feet or getting tangled around my legs. I only wobbled occasionally now, partly from being tired. I bet I'd have a much harder time though, if I didn't already know how to cross-country ski. I wished this were just another day out in the woods, having fun, exploring with my friends.

But it wasn't. It was a race against time.

"Hike, hike, hike!" I called to Raven, urging her to go faster. When she picked up the pace, everyone else did, too.

And where the heck had Roy gone, anyway? I thought for sure he'd double back to see why we'd lagged behind.

Raven and I took the lead. I tried to imagine what we'd find at the crash site. Warden Kate tied up? Hurt? Karl with the lynx in a trap? Or worse, would the poacher have already killed it for its beautiful pelt?

Looking up, I noticed the puffy gray clouds in the distance had doubled.

The next time we stop, I'll check the weather again, I promised myself.

Ahead of us was a right turn, just as we entered the thick woods again. From here we'd start heading down the other side of the mountain. As we got closer, I realized the turn was more curved than I'd realized, hairpin sharp, with nine-foot-tall rocks on either side.

"Gee, gee!" I hollered, so everyone would hear. I wanted to be sure Wynter started turning in time.

We slowed a bit as the trail became narrower and more winding. A large, yellow, diamond-shaped sign with an "S" handpainted on it hung on a post just before the next turn.

S-curve, I thought, dragging my weight to get Raven to slow. "Gee, gee!"

Raven made the turn, but I had to help so I didn't ski up over the ridge of snow on the edge of the trail and run into a rock.

"Haw, haw!" I called again. *Whew!* I grinned. This was actually kind of fun!

Coming out of that S-curve, I was surprised to see another on the left. "Gee, gee!" I was beginning to feel like a broken record! But I had to be sure everyone behind me knew about it in time. I called again over my shoulder. "Gee, gee!"

Raven barked in earnest as she suddenly tugged me forward, fast.

"Whoa!" I called. "Whoa!"

Right away, I noticed two things. One, a bright red snowmobile lay on its side, the motor still running. And two, the driver lay in a heap in the snowbank alongside a boulder.

Not moving.

It was Roy!

CHAPTER 27

*The US Fish and Wildlife Service listed lynx
as threatened in March 2000. Human activity in
lynx's favorite habitat has played a role
in their declining numbers.*

"Roy!" I half-cried, half-screamed his name.

Unclipping myself from Raven, I ran toward my friend.

Roy lay on his right side, arms and legs outstretched in every direction. Somehow, the impact had popped his helmet off his head. His snowmobile, still running, lay on its side at the top of a two-foot-high snowbank. A boulder loomed behind it. The sled he'd been towing had flown into the woods, our gear scattered everywhere.

Had he hit the banking with the snowmobile? Had Roy been thrown into the rock?

Wynter jumped off the sled before it stopped moving. Summer rushed over to throw the snow hook down and step on it before racing to Roy's side.

Wynter beat me by a toenail, falling to her knees beside my snowmobile-loving friend. Raven tried to squeeze under her arm to see him, but Wynter gently pushed her dog back.

"Don't roll him over!" I cried.

"I wasn't going to!" she yelled back. Summer put a hand on her arm to calm her.

Packrat fell to his knees on the other side of Roy, holding Moose's harness.

"He kept whining and tugging to get over here," he explained. "Actually, wrapped his leg around mine."

The four of us looked Roy up and down without touching him, searching for bruising, swelling, oddly shaped areas, all signs of a possible broken bone. We checked his breathing and looked for any cuts he might have. I didn't know about Wynter and Summer, but Packrat, Roy, and I had learned this in a CPR class my parents had insisted we take at the fire station.

Reaching into a large inside pocket, Packrat pulled out a first-aid kit.

There were no injuries that we could see, but what about what we couldn't see?

Packrat let Moose go forward just enough to sniff Roy and see him for himself. Clutching my arm, Summer whispered, "Is he . . . is he . . ."

Before any of us could stop him, Moose leaned over to give Roy a great, big, slobbery lick from his neck to his forehead. Packrat pulled Moose back, putting his arms around his neck and murmuring in his ear.

Quiet moans came from Roy. I leaned in a bit, but I couldn't hear a word over the running snowmobile.

"Turn that thing off!" I barked at no one in particular.

Summer scrambled to take care of it.

"Roy?" Why wouldn't Wynter get out of my way! I itched to push her aside. Roy was my friend!

More weak groans from Roy. Turning himself over gingerly, he lay on his back for a second, looking up at the now-gray sky. Wincing a bit, he rolled to one side and tried to sit up.

"What's with all the freaked-out faces? Geez. You all act like you've never seen anybody get thrown from their snowmobile before!"

Wynter started fussing over him, telling him he shouldn't get up yet. Where did it hurt? Lay back. Could he move his legs? His arms?

Roy gave her one of his furrowed-brow, what-the-heck looks. He moved his arms, then his legs. Squinting at her now, he said, "You happy, Wynter Nightingale? I'll be all right!"

Wynter froze. Roy's eyes widened. "Did I get it right?"

"No." The sides of Wynter's mouth curved upward. "I'm just impressed you know about Florence Nightingale."

Roy frowned again and waved her off. "I read stuff! And by the way, that was a joke, not a guess."

"Well, since you're hurt and woozy, I'll let you get away with it," she shot back.

Getting one elbow underneath himself, Roy pushed up into a sitting position, then carefully started to stand, as if he were trying out all his parts. Halfway up, his knees wobbled a bit. Wynter moved to his right and I went to his left, to support him.

"My snowmobile?" he asked, his voice stronger.

"You can't drive it!" Summer's eyes were shiny. She put out her hand toward him. "Look at you!" She then swung it toward his machine. "Look at that!"

Packrat shook his head sadly. "Sorry. It's not going anywhere, Roy. I think it's totaled."

Roy stood tall, shaking off Wynter and me. He walked to his snowmobile, leaned over it, and grabbed hold of both handlebars. Tugging it, he tried to rock the snowmobile into an upright position. Even though he seemed steady on his feet now, I could tell he didn't have the strength. I took one handlebar, Packrat took the other, and we rolled it back on its skis.

One quick look told us all we needed to know. The handlebars were twisted at an odd angle and one of the skis had broken. It wasn't going anywhere.

"Sorry, Roy," Wynter said.

Roy kicked his machine in frustration. "Owww!" he leaned on the hood and lowered his chin to his chest. "Stupid snowmobiler!"

Wait. What?

Remembering the reckless yellow snowmobile, I asked, "You were run off the trail?"

"You think I did this to myself?"

Oops. Yes, actually—my first thought when I'd seen him lying there was that he'd gone too fast around the corner.

Roy put his hands on his head, his shoulders slumping. "I didn't even hear him coming."

"We barely got off the trail in time, too," Summer told him.

Roy put his right hand on the back of his neck and rolled his head around. "I swerved, saw the snowbank coming for my face, and bailed."

Packrat winced. "Owww."

"*Owww* doesn't begin to cover it." Roy grimaced. "You all seem to have survived the jerk passing you."

"If we hadn't stopped to take that phone call, we might not have heard him either, and we'd probably look a lot like you right now." I'd have to fill Roy in on Karl's call later.

"The dogs?" Roy craned his neck to check on them.

"All good," Wynter assured him. "It's you we're worried about."

"Now how will I ride?" Roy groaned.

"If we tie your plastic sled to the back of my dogsled, and move a bale of straw there, you can sit in the basket in front of me," Wynter suggested.

"Good idea!" Summer went to take Roy's arm, but he pulled it back.

Hitching his chin toward me, he said, "I'll try that skidooring thing now."

I laughed a little to lighten the mood but watched his face closely. "Skijoring. And yeah. I don't think so."

Roy groaned. "I don't want to be a passenger!"

Packrat spoke hesitantly. "I hate to be the voice of reason, but maybe we should turn back? What if you have a concussion? Some internal—"

"I'm fine!" Roy grumbled.

I had to admit, his voice sounded stronger, and a little embarrassed by all the attention.

"I'm telling you. It was a controlled bail. The snowbank just turned out to be a little harder than I thought."

"Let me run through the concussion symptoms," I suggested. "Then we'll decide."

"Geez," Roy glared at me. "One little eight-hour CPR and first-aid course and you think you're a doctor now."

Ha! He hadn't said no, which meant he'd let me.

Packrat waved Summer over and the two of them started picking up Roy's gear, piling it back in his black sled.

"First," I said, drawing a line in the snow with the heel of my boot, "walk this line, heel to toe." Roy did it perfectly without hesitating or wobbling.

"Say, Peter Piper picked a peck of pickled peppers." When Roy didn't stumble over his words or pause, I asked, "Who's the president?"

"Joe Biden."

"Do you feel sick?"

"Just over my snowmobile." Roy glanced toward Moose. "And the slobbery kiss."

I laughed. "Your memory is good. Headache?"

Roy bent down to pat Moose on his neck. I swear Moose tried to crawl into his coat. With his head up against Moose's, he said, "It's good." When Wynter and I didn't say anything, he insisted, "It is!"

I held up four fingers. "How many?"

"Five." Roy gave Moose one last pat and stood.

Wynter and I had frozen in place.

"Oh, c'mon you guys!" Roy threw his hands in the air and stormed to the dogsled. "I'm kidding!" Climbing in the basket, he crossed his arms and waited. When none of us moved, he groaned. "Four. There were four fingers, okay? But I get it. I took the course too, you know. You have to 'monitor me,' " he said, holding up both hands and making air quotes. He crossed his arms again. "So, let's just go, okay?"

Wynter rushed to fuss over him again, getting him a blanket, making room for him amid the gear stored there. I couldn't tell if his ears were red from all the attention, or from being mad at us for making him ride in the basket. Wynter started to zip up the bag around him, but he pushed her hands away. "You're wasting time!" he told her.

Packrat stepped in. "He's got a point. The trailhead is only five minutes away. It'd be dumb to go back now. Let's just find a place to get off the trail completely. It won't add much time."

I hooked Raven up to my belt again, then looked up. Gray clouds covered the sky now. It looked like those snow squalls were on the way.

"Hike, hike!" I called. Raven took off.

Something didn't feel right about this trip anymore. If we weren't already practically at the trailhead taking us to the downed plane, I'd be turning around to head back.

Because for the first time, I felt a little scared.

"This is it," I told my friends, minutes later.

The all-terrain trail veered off to the left, but the crash site was marked with a diamond-shaped yellow sign with a plane symbol on it. I could tell that tons of snowmobilers had traveled here to hike up to the site, because the trail groomers had plowed out a mini parking lot. Wynter drove her sled in there.

Roy stepped out of the sled's basket easily. He looked better, but I still wanted him to take it easy until we got him home.

"I don't think we should take Wynter's sled up there," I said, glancing at Roy.

"Agreed," Wynter said. "The dogs would make too much noise."

"We really should stake it out, so we have the element of surprise on our side."

"Okay, okay," Roy grumbled. "I get it. I'll stay."

Summer looked at the trail, then at Roy. "I'll stay, too."

"No," Roy said firmly. "Look, Cooper might need all of you up there. I still don't have a headache, no signs of dizziness. I'm good." When we all hesitated, he threw his hands in the air. "C'mon! If someone has to stay with the dogs, I'm the logical choice."

"I don't want us to be up there long," I reassured him. "I want to hike up, see if Warden Kate is there, or the lynx, then we'll come back, and go home."

"Riiiiiight," Roy said.

"Uh-huh," Packrat echoed.

Summer gave Wynter a hint of a smile. "It's never easy with us."

Wynter gave Roy a list of to-dos for the dogs, like laying out straw for them to rest on, and telling him how much food to feed them. Packrat checked his pockets. First-aid kit? Check. Phone? Check.

"Compass?" I asked.

"Check."

"Flashlight?" Summer suggested. "Just in case."

"Check."

The four of us stepped onto the trail. But then I had a worry-thought.

"Roy." I turned to him. "Just in case, we're hiking up to the point where you see a bunch of flags, a big piece of plane body, and the giant wheels on their axle. There are pieces everywhere, but that's the main place for visitors to pay their respects. From there, we're hooking a left and heading northwest, and there's no trail. We'll be looking for a shed-sized, rotted building with a ring of rocks for a campfire pit. I explored it with my parents a few years ago. I have a feeling it's where the warden thinks the poacher's base is."

"Got it," Roy said.

Turning to leave, I looked at the upward climb ahead of us. Raven appeared from nowhere, looking to me for the signal to go. "I don't know . . ." I told her.

"It's okay." Wynter patted her head. "She can be very stealthy."

I hoped so. Because I had no idea what or who was waiting for us up there.

CHAPTER 28

Lynx kittens are playful, but their rough-and-tumble
wrestling is really practice for learning how to hunt.

The snow was halfway to our knees, and the trail underneath was rocky, slick, and uphill. After fifteen minutes, I was huffing and puffing. And I wasn't the only one. Packrat, Wynter, and Summer were breathing hard, too. The only one who wasn't, was Raven. "I need a break," I said, partly for me and partly for my friends.

Packrat pulled a bottle of water from his inside pocket and handed it to me before reaching for another. Summer practically downed her own bottle in one gulp.

"We're almost there," Wynter said, putting her water bottle to her lips.

More mixed signals! Wynter obviously knew the area, yet she continued to help us look for Warden Kate and the lynx. So, were she and her mom in on this pelts-to-Canada thing or not?

Packrat pulled a flat disk from a pocket. Pushing on the middle, he popped up the sides, poured water in it, and put the little bowl down for Raven to take a drink.

Five minutes, and we were on our way again.

The trail got a little steeper, but the snow wasn't as deep. I readjusted my backpack as we crested a hill. Before us lay a round piece of metal, three feet in diameter and about six feet long, sticking out of the snow. The edges on both sides were jagged and torn. The outside was dirty-white. Inside, wires dangled from the ceiling.

A few feet away and off to our right stood two tires taller than us, the axle between them still intact, black paint rusting off.

We'd reached the main site of the crash.

"So, this is the memorial?" Summer turned in a circle. "There aren't many plane pieces."

"These are just the biggest pieces," Packrat told her. "The wreckage is scattered up and down this side of the mountain. There are tons of smaller pieces, under the snow. But this is the spot where most of it lies."

I pointed northwest. "We need to go that way, off-trail now. The little camp is just over the ridge. We'll have to be quiet so we can stake out—"

"Stakeout!" Packrat cried. Digging around a large inner pocket, he pulled out his camo poncho. "Do you have yours?"

"Yes!" I dropped my backpack and dug around inside until I pulled out my own.

"What about us?" Wynter asked.

I pulled out two small, square packages and offered them to the girls. "These rain ponchos aren't painted like ours, but they're white and will help hide your bright coats."

We put on our camo and headed up the mountain, walking slower now, knowing how close we were. We didn't want anyone to hear us coming.

Seeing the shed-like, skinny brown building through the trees, I put a finger to my lips. Warily, we inched behind a longer but slightly smaller tube like the one before. Slipping behind it, poncho hoods on, the four of us looked over the mangled plane part onto the campsite.

Someone had fixed up the shed, putting plywood over the holes. A tent was set up, too, snow all around it like our own winter forts. A campfire, burning very low, told us someone had been here not too long ago. Wire cages sat on more cages, four across and two or three high. I couldn't see into every single one, but I could make out rabbits, minks, martens, and two red foxes.

A clothesline rope stretched between two trees at the back of the site. Instead of clothes, it held furs of every color and size. I recognized rabbit, mink, fox, fisher, and otter. There was even a bear pelt tacked to the side of the little shed!

I fisted my hands in frustration. I had no problem with trapping or hunting, if the season and limit rules were followed. In fact, those rules were there for a good reason. But there were too many pelts here to be legal! And every single one of those animals had been caught out of their trapping season!

No doubt about it. We had found our illegal poacher.

But not Warden Kate.

"Cooper?" Packrat looked at me. "No people. No snowmobile. Nobody's home."

A loud bark from the campsite made us look toward a top cage where a red fox looked back at us. Then the cage under it wiggled a bit, and when the animal leaned against the mesh front, I swear my blood began to boil. I knew that tannish-gray fur.

The lynx kitten was here!

It took everything I had to stay put and not bolt over to check on it right this second.

"We're not leaving without the lynx," I said. "We're not leaving any of them trapped like this."

I'd said it, but I wasn't sure how we'd do it.

"Let's release them all!" Packrat's eyes twinkled. "Imagine the look on the poacher's face when he gets back."

"No!" Wynter looked horrified at the thought. "In and out! We take the lynx, sure, but then we go home! This guy spent hours, days, laying traps for these animals, taking the pelts and drying them. He isn't going to say, 'Oh well, they got the best of me. Guess I'll pack up now.' He'll hunt us down—target us! Trap us!"

Packrat and I stared at her. "Trap us," I repeated. "Trap . . ."

My mind whirled with possibilities! Packrat, Summer, and I shared determined looks and nodded.

Wynter looked at us all suspiciously. "What am I missing?"

I grinned at her. "That poacher can't trap us if we trap him first!"

We had to hurry. I knew the poacher would be back sooner rather than later for two reasons. One, his campfire was still hot. This must be home base for sure. Warden Kate had mentioned that he might be collecting traps and selling off all the evidence before his trial. I'd bet he'd been in and out of this camp all day. And two, he'd left his pelts out for anyone to take instead of locking them up.

My first idea had been to take one of the poacher's own leg snares and put it where he'd be sure to walk into it and get caught. I thought it'd be what my mom called poetic justice. He wouldn't be able follow us, and he'd be trapped until we sent someone back to catch him red-handed in the middle of the evidence that would lock him away.

But when we'd searched the little brown shed, we discovered a gold mine of trapping gear. Gear I'd never even seen before! Some of it was illegal, too. No wonder Warden Kate couldn't find any evidence at his house. Every single bit of it was stored here! We were so mad, we decided to go big! Not just one trap, but a bunch of traps.

Booby traps!

After carefully placing and camouflaging them, mostly with snow, a frustrated Wynter reminded us it could take the guy hours to accidentally trip one. She was right, too. So, that's when I decided to lay the bait.

After releasing the snowshoe hares back into the wild, we carefully placed the cages on their sides in the middle of our minefield, doors hanging open. We had just barely finished when we heard the roar of a snowmobile.

He was coming.

Calling Raven, we ran back behind the piece of plane and waited.

A yellow snowmobile came screaming through the woods to park next to the shed. I groaned. The driver and the poacher did know each other! Were they partners?

The driver got up and pulled off the helmet. We gasped as one.

The yellow snowmobiler and Thomas Scott were one and the same! How had I not guessed this before?

I glanced at Wynter. This guy had waved at her mom, twice. She gave no sign of knowing him.

Seeing the empty cage on the back of his snowmobile, my eyes narrowed.

Warden Kate had called it: This guy was collecting all his traps!

The poacher shook his head and ran a hand back and forth over his shaggy hair. Then he ran it down his face.

I knew the second he spotted the tipped-over empty rabbit cages, because his hand froze somewhere between his nose and his chin as he stared hard at it. Looking back to the cages full of animals, I could see the wheels turning in his head. Counting.

Dropping the helmet, Thomas Scott stormed toward the pile.

Wait for it. Wait for it.

Scott's foot caught on the trip wire we'd run between two trees. His eyes widened right before he landed face-first in the snow.

Packrat snickered, and even Wynter cracked a smile.

"What the . . ." Jumping up, he looked around, his face covered in snow. Wiping it off with his sleeve, he walked more slowly toward the cages.

Snap!

"Owww!" He hopped to the left. Snap! He hopped backwards. *Snap! Snap!*

One by one he triggered all the steel animal traps we'd laid out under the snow.

I had to hide my laughter behind both gloved hands. The guy looked like he was dancing a jig in the middle of the woods—and Packrat was videotaping it!

Snap! Snap! Snappity-snap!

SNAP!

"Owww!" Scott stopped dancing. He fell on his butt and lifted his foot. A large steel trap had caught his boot tip. I had one second of feeling bad for him, until I remembered this guy had trapped tons of animals, way more than allowed. Animals he was supposed to leave alone because there were so few left in the state.

Darn! It didn't look like the toothy trap had broken through his boot. The guy probably wore steel-toe boots. But that was okay. Up until now, we had just been messing with him anyway, paying him back for all the animals he'd poached. We needed him to trip another hidden wire, which would release the big trap, the one to keep him here until the wardens could collect him with all the evidence.

Remembering how the wire ran left to right between two trees right before the empty traps, I rubbed my hands together in anticipation.

"Whoever you are, I'm coming for you!" Scott screamed as he struggled to stand after releasing his boot from the steel trap.

Limping slightly, he headed for the bait. Suddenly, he froze from head to toe. The only thing left moving was his eyes.

"What's he doing?" Summer's whisper sounded a little nervous.

The poacher turned in place, studying the ground everywhere. His boots didn't leave the spot he was on. It was almost as if he was afraid to . . .

Move.

The snow.

The rest of our tracks!

"I think," I told Summer, "he just figured out we're still here."

CHAPTER 29

Lynx are not fast runners. They need to be sneaky to catch their prey, sometimes lying in wait for hours, letting their meal come close enough before giving chase.

The poacher's eyes had landed on our tracks—the ones that led from the empty rabbit cages to our hiding spot.

"Come out, come out, wherever you are!" he called in a singsong voice, taking one cautious step forward.

C'mon, c'mon, I pleaded in my head, *just a couple more steps!*

A phone rang. Scott stopped a foot from the trigger to pull a phone out of his pocket. I groaned as he barked into it, "I'm busy. Be quick!"

For a split second, I thought the phone would distract him enough for us to sprint to a new hiding spot. Unfortunately, the guy was smarter than I thought. He kept suspiciously scanning the woods as the person on the other end of the call talked.

Just three more steps!

The poacher's face changed from angry to frustrated. "But . . . but . . . but."

Scott paused to listen. Whatever the other person said made him kick the tower of cages closest to him. The tower teetered, and the fox in the cage on top crouched, its eyes wild.

I heard a low growl and looked at Raven. But Wynter shook her head and tipped it toward Packrat. His hands fisted up, his body tense, he gave another growl. Summer put a hand on his shoulder to calm him down before he did something crazy. But I understood his rage.

Our lynx was in the middle of that teetering cage pile.

The lynx backed up as far as it could to the back corners of its jail cell, its head and shoulders lowering to the floor.

"I told ya, I'm not giving away my location for no one," the poacher argued. "Not even for you. This spot's perfect for trapping out of season. Other than a few people hiking to the memorial, it's deserted this time of year. No one thinks to come all the way out here. Not even the wardens."

Ha! I thought. *Little did he know they were on to him.*

Thomas Scott had stopped again to listen.

"Yes, yes, I'll sell you the pelts now. But I'm not doing it cheap after everything I've been through. You better not disappoint me like the first buyer did, or I'll cut you out, too. I'm sorry I ever took the lynx job. You know what they would do to me, if by some miracle they found proof of everything? The maximum penalty is something like twenty-five thousand dollars and a hundred and eighty days in jail! But I know that warden would make an example of me and charge me with more! Maybe take away my license and my trapping equipment—"

Scott listened some more.

"Yeah, you're right, it's better than dumping them in the woods. I've been sledding up and down the trail and through these woods for two whole days, collecting everything I can." He glanced at the live animals in the cages. "I got the lynx kitten, too. Managed to grab it when everyone went to the lake to get their stupid dogsled rides. It was easy, with it being hungry and all." He rolled his eyes. "Yes, it's alive. Why the heck does everyone want it alive?"

Everyone?

"Your money will help me lay low for a while," he continued.

I tried to lean closer, to get some idea of who he was talking to.

The guy was walking in circles now, and those circles were getting wider each time.

C'mon. C'mon. Trip the wire!

"Why are you so worried?"

He stopped walking and talking to listen to the person on the other end. The four of us groaned softly.

Summer had her head in her mittens. "I can't watch!"

"Kids?" Thomas Scott's eyes shot back to our tracks in the snow. "Wait, yeah. There were kids on the trail. I passed them. But they . . ."

The poacher's eyes narrowed as he glanced toward our hiding spot. Then a smile slowly formed on his face.

My heart raced so fast I thought it'd burst. *He figured it out!*

"There's something I have to take care of now," Scott explained into the phone. "I'll meet you at the old bridge tomorrow morning with your pelts. I'll include that lynx alive for another thousand dollars. Maybe I'll have another surprise or two, as well. Bring cash."

I didn't think. I just knew two things.

One, I needed that guy to keep the caller on the phone, so we'd know once and for all who wanted the lynx so badly.

And two, I needed him to spring the last trap.

So I stood up. And stared coolly at him.

Okay, so I shook in my boots while I stared coolly. And not from the cold.

Packrat hissed, "Get down!" He reached around Wynter to grab my poncho and tug. But it was too late. The guy had seen me.

"Cooper?" Wynter whispered frantically. She was struggling to hold Raven back from rushing the guy. "What are you doing?"

The poacher saw me in spite of my camouflage. He took a step toward me. Raven began barking, the hair on the back of her shoulders standing up. Scott paused. Whoever was on the phone was still talking a mile a minute. I had to keep them on the line!

Lifting my chin, I held out my hand and gave him a come-and-get-me motion.

Packrat muttered, "Oh, what the heck," and stood up beside me. Wynter and Summer followed.

The poacher's eyes turned a cold and steely gray. He took another step toward us, scanning the ground again for more booby traps. He was trying to figure out what we were up to.

"I hope you know what you're doing!" Packrat whispered.

"Hey, jerk face!" I hollered. "Afraid of a coupla kids?"

Thomas lowered the phone and roared. One step. Two steps. His boot tip caught the wire, pulling it up out of the snow. He must have felt the tug, because he froze, his mouth forming an O, but no sound came out. For a second, nothing happened. The world seemed to pause. Scott began to smile.

Whoosh! A huge net released from the tree branches above. Watching it fan out like a parachute on the way down to land on the poacher's head was the coolest thing I'd seen in weeks!

"Yeah!" I hollered, punching a fist in the air in celebration.

"I can't believe that actually worked!" Wynter said, grabbing my sleeve as the four of us rushed forward.

The poacher wiggled and jiggled and pulled at the net, trying to get it off. But the more he struggled, the more he got tangled in it. Suddenly, his feet went out from under him and he fell down hard. Roaring now, he kept wiggling. I let him.

Raven raced ahead of us to dance around the heap of net and poacher, barking and nipping at his heels. Packrat pulled a couple of tent stakes from his pocket, along with a hammer. "This will keep him in one place!" he said, pounding them through the net into the snow and frozen ground.

Seeing the glint of something silver under the netting, I quickly put my hand in to pull it out.

"No!" the guy hollered, as I put his phone to my ear.

"What the heck is going on?" a familiar voice said. "Thomas? Thomas!"

Packrat glanced up at me, hit the last stake in, then did a double take. He must have seen the shock and anger on my face because I sure could feel it boiling in my chest.

My narrowed eyes slid to Wynter.

"What?" she whispered.

I handed her the phone. "Say hello to your mother."

CHAPTER 30

Female lynx and kittens hunt together as a team.
They walk in a line, with one flushing out the prey and
another catching it.

Wynter's hand shook as she put Thomas Scott's phone to her ear. The trapped poacher hollered about his rights and how we'd be in so much trouble if we didn't release him from the net immediately.

Rights! What made him think he deserved rights after poaching wildlife? He'd broken every law in the book! I wanted to kick him like he'd kicked the cage.

But I was better than that.

Besides, my anger was directed at someone else right now.

"Mom?" Wynter whispered the word. Her eyes widened, then narrowed. "What am *I* doing here?" She gave a half-bark, half-laugh. "What are *you* doing calling this jerk? You told me this wasn't a working trip!" She listened again, turned away from us, and said, "It's too late, Mom. Cooper recognized your voice." Wynter began pacing back and forth, just like the poacher had. We all listened, even Scott.

"After I defended you to my friends? 'No way is my mother involved in the poaching or the buying,' I said. 'My mother would never—' " Wynter threw her free hand on top of her head. "*What? You're blaming me for this mess?* If you'd just been honest!"

I heard Lisa's voice through the phone—not the words, but the feelings in them. I expected pleading or begging or worry. After all, we'd just netted a dangerous trapper in the middle of nowhere with hundreds, no thousands of dollars' worth of pelts on the line. My mom would have been worried sick about me!

Not Lisa, apparently. Her voice was frosty—angry—and she was issuing demands of some kind.

"Fine! Don't worry!" Suddenly, Wynter's face got splotchy. Her eyes, shiny. "Yeah, I'll come back with the dogs, but not because you ordered me to! First, we're letting all the animals go."

Lisa's voice rose a notch.

Wynter smiled, and I sensed she was trying to hurt her mom where it hurt most.

"Oh, believe it, Mom. Every. Single. One."

Wynter hung up. "Oooooooooo!" She threw the phone to me. "My own mother."

Ducking her head, she took the back of her mitten and rubbed the end of her red nose. Eyes shining with tears, she turned away. "How could she put me in this position?" she muttered. "Why didn't she trust me?"

Packrat, Summer, and I watched silently as she struggled with this knowledge of her mom. At first, I'd been so angry, I'd wanted to put Wynter in the net with Scott and leave her there. Clearly, though, she was upset at her mother's involvement. She'd had no clue the poacher and her mother knew each other. I couldn't imagine finding out my mom was an illegal fur trader.

There was a saying: *Keep your friends close and your enemies closer.* I wasn't sure which one Wynter was anymore, but we needed her to get us home, so she'd be staying with us.

For now.

Packrat pulled out two pairs of heavy work gloves and handed me one. Switching to those from my soft winter gloves, I checked the cages over. These animals had been captured and some were on edge and scared. Packrat's gloves could save me from losing a finger. Or at the very least, getting bitten.

The poacher began to howl and roar. Some of the animals stirred in their cages from nervousness. Knowing they'd been trapped in this neck of the woods within the last few days, I felt pretty good about letting them go here.

I inspected the cages. "Looks like a simple release," I said. Packrat and I each lifted the ends of a trap holding a growling raccoon. "Let's start at the bottom of the food chain."

Wynter agreed, but asked, "Do you think they'll just bolt when we open the doors?"

"We've watched Warden Kate release animals before," Packrat told her, while shrugging out of his coat to throw it over the cage. "They usually take off without a backward glance."

Scott let out another bellow.

Packrat and I carried the raccoon's cage to the tree line and set it down. Wynter took off her hat and scarf, putting them on Packrat. My friend's ears turned red as she adjusted the scarf. "I don't want you to freeze."

I flipped the latch and we all moved behind the covered cage. I swung open the door from behind.

Nothing happened.

"This might take longer than we thought," Packrat said.

"We don't have a lot of time, though." I gently lifted the back end of the cage.

Two furry, triangular ears and a black nose poked out and wiggled. Suddenly, with a chitter-chatter of excitement, the raccoon took off.

Wynter and Packrat brought over the ermine next. It didn't waste a second, scurrying away in a flash!

One by one we let them go. Packrat and Wynter had just picked up the last cage holding a red fox when Packrat stopped. "Did you hear something?"

I listened. "No."

Packrat nodded. "That's just it. It's too quiet."

The net bundle wiggled, but the poacher stayed eerily quiet. Hesitantly, I took a step toward him, but paused when I heard a swishing sound.

The dogs!

Roy was standing on the runners, his face screwed up in concentration.

"Whoa!" he cried. "Whoa!"

But the dogs didn't stop until they met up with Wynter, who had put down the fox's cage to run toward them. Falling to her knees, she greeted the lead dog with a hug around the neck. "Did you all take good care of Roy for me?" she cooed to River.

Raven raced over to greet all five dogs, nose to nose, as if to say *What took you so long?*

"Aw!" Roy took it all in. "It looks like I missed all the fun! You guys were taking too long. I started to get worried, so I packed up and got the dogs ready, figuring you'd come tearing out of the woods, yelling that we had to make a run for it. After fifteen more minutes, the dogs got wicked restless, and I couldn't hold River back anymore. I figured they sensed you were in danger or needed help or something, so I planned to save the day."

Packrat said, "Everything's under control."

"Really?" Roy pointed to Thomas Scott. "Do you always let your bad guys get away?"

I whirled in time to see Thomas Scott's hand shoot out of the netting, the sharp edge of a knife glinting in his hand. How had I missed it? The poacher was trying to cut himself free! Of course, a poacher would have a knife in his pocket. Duh!

"Quick!" I hollered, "Packrat, take Roy and pound in a few more stakes around—"

In a few quick steps, Roy stormed to the tangled mess of man and net. He kicked the poacher's hand, sending the knife flying. Scott roared, and roll-lunged toward Roy, but my friend easily danced out of reach.

Packrat picked up the knife and put it in one of his coat pockets. But we could see that the poacher had already made cuts in the netting. How long would it hold him now?

"C'mon Roy," Packrat said, "help me with the stakes. It might by us some time. "Summer, let's release the fox!" I urged. "Then we'll all meet at the dogsled!"

Wynter ran to her dogs. Once the fox was released, Summer and I hurried back to the lynx cage. The kitten looked at me suspiciously through the wire mesh.

"Sorry, buddy," I said, in as calm a voice as I could, even though my heart raced. Packrat appeared at my side to cover the cage with his coat. "We can't let you go just yet," I murmured as we race-walked to the sled. "We're taking you back to Warden Kate; she'll know what to do so we can safely put you back into the wild."

I wished once again we'd found Warden Kate here. This would have been so much easier with her help.

We loaded the cage into the basket on Wynter's sled. She dug out a blanket to cover it and gave a shivering Packrat his coat back.

Roy came trotting over. "I checked out that yellow snowmobile. I think your poacher guy has the keys on him. I can't start it without them." He looked to the lynx cage in the dogsled, then to Wynter. "Looks like I'm riding on the back with you."

Wynter grinned. "I thought you'd never try it!"

"Wait a minute." Roy's eyes narrowed as he looked between Packrat and Wynter. "Is he wearing your hat?"

"I'm coming for you!" Scott yelled, his arm breaking free of the netting, like he was reaching up through the ice on a lake for a lifeline. We all watched, ready to run. Instead, he seemed to become way more tangled as he struggled, and I breathed a sigh of relief. I knew that if he got the chance, he'd do just what he promised; break free and chase after us to get back the lynx and pelts. Hopefully, our head start would have us with the wardens by the time he caught up.

I clipped my line to Raven's harness. I could hear the clicks of Packrat's and Summer's as well.

"Let's go!" I hollered.

"Let's go!" Wynter echoed, as she pulled in her brake.

Those were the best words I'd heard in a long time.

CHAPTER 31

Lynx are naturally very calm animals.

About an hour later, we took a quick break to catch our breath and eat something. Every one of us kept an ear toward the trail, listening for Thomas Scott. We'd already passed Roy's broken snowmobile, stopping only long enough to tie the black sled to it, since it was now empty of supplies. We were getting to the bottom of our food and had a little less than half our water left. The dogs had eaten the meal Wynter brought for them, and we'd left behind the wet straw they'd rested on at the base of the trail. So the little bit of gear we still had, we put on the dog sled. Just before leaving there, I saw Roy lay a hand on the seat of his snowmobile, and I swear I heard him talk to it, vowing to return for it soon.

Now, we were on the stretch of trail where we'd run into the moose.

Wynter checked each dog, giving them water. I did the same with Roy, which annoyed him no end. A good sign my friend was fine.

"How are you?" I asked. "Any headache?"

Roy snorted. "I'm tough. No headache. Just a little sore all over."

"That's 'cause you have a hard head!" Summer told him.

The sky was totally overcast and the dampness in the air told me it would snow soon. Would we make it home before dark? What would we find when we did?

I'd wanted to ask Wynter about her mom, but I got the sense she was still struggling to sort it all out in her head. The stuff she'd said before, about how angry poachers can get—did she know this firsthand?

The dogs were getting tired. They still wiggled as Wynter moved among them, but all four paws stayed on the ground now.

"I offered to help her, but she wouldn't let me," Summer quietly said to me as we stood side by side, wolfing down the peanut butter and jelly sandwiches we'd brought. "She hasn't said a word since we hit the trail again."

"What's going on?" Roy grumbled. "What happened back there? She wouldn't even take the bait when I threw out Wynter Crystal!"

"Thomas Scott was talking on the phone, trying to sell the pelts, when we took him down with the net," I explained. I looked at Wynter's sled, which not only held the lynx, but as many pelts as we could fit. "He dropped the phone—"

Packrat interrupted, "Cooper picked it up—"

"And it was Wynter's mom," Summer finished.

Roy raised an eyebrow, but he didn't interrupt.

I tipped my head toward Wynter. "She was wicked upset. Yelled at her mom, told her there was no way she'd do what she asked."

Roy leaned forward. "What'd she ask?"

"I don't know," I told him. "But whatever it was, it made her cry."

We'd all decided I should try to call Warden Kate as soon as I had a signal. I'd lost it the minute we'd left Piehl Mountain. And even though I checked every five minutes, I didn't have enough bars until we'd traveled another forty-five minutes.

Stopping Raven, I looked again at my phone. Two bars! Quickly, I dialed Warden Kate's number.

"Hello . . ."

Yes! "Warden Kate?"

". . . the person you are trying to reach is not available. This voicemail box is full."

"Aaaaahhhhh!" I cried. "Now what?" I looked to Packrat.

"I know she hasn't really listened to us so far," Packrat hesitated, "but what about Warden Penny? Maybe she heard from Warden Kate while we were out of range."

He was right, but still I hesitated. I knew calling her meant all our parents would get involved. "Yeah," I said. "All right, here goes nothing."

"Cooper!" Warden Penny answered before the first ring stopped. "Where are you? We're all so worried! You went to the crash site, didn't you?"

"We're heading back," I reassured her. "We've got the lynx, and some pelts as proof of Thomas Scott's poaching, but I couldn't find Warden Kate."

"She's fine! I told you, she followed a different lead." Warden Penny sighed. "Cooper, I take full responsibility for this. I should have listened to you and worked with you in the first place, just like Warden Kate does. It's just . . . I don't know . . . I'm not as good at working with kids."

"We get that a lot," I told her.

"So, let me help you bring the lynx and pelts in."

"We're halfway home," I said. "But there's more. We, um, left the poacher tangled in a net—"

"You what?" The warden's voice had gotten very quiet. "He was there?"

"It's a long story," I quickly told her. "And there's more."

I heard Roy and Wynter coming up behind us. Watching Wynter as she dragged her heel and whoa-ed the dogs to get them to stop, I waffled. Did I tell Warden Penny what I knew? Or wait for Warden Kate? But what if Penny got into trouble somehow because she didn't know?

"I think Wynter's mom, Lisa, is working with the poacher. They're planning to meet tomorrow so she can buy the pelts."

Silence came through the line so thick, I thought I'd lost my connection. I looked at the phone. Nope. I had three bars.

"Warden?"

The dogs started barking like crazy, as Wynter and Roy hopped off the sled to check on them and their lines.

"Warden?" I tried again.

"Cooper, sorry, I hear you. Good job! That's just what we needed! I'm on my way, okay? I'll try to reach Warden Kate and advise her about Lisa."

A low humming filled the air. As it got louder and louder, I turned in circles looking for it. Packrat looked up, too, shielding his eyes. Roy and Summer and Wynter saw us and did the same.

It was hard to spot at first, against the gray sky. A small, white, two-seater plane in the distance was closing in on us. I asked the warden, "Did you send a plane?"

"No."

The plane roared over us. The tint on the windshield kept me from seeing the pilot. Banking, it came back around to waggle its wings before flying off.

"Cooper?" Warden Penny brought my attention back to the phone. "Why do you ask?"

"Because if somebody's looking for us, they just found us."

CHAPTER 32

If a trapper accidentally catches a lynx, Maine law requires them not to release it, and to report it immediately. This way, biologists can check the lynx over and treat any injuries before letting it go.

"Cooper, I didn't send a plane." Rustling sounds and the slamming of a door came through the phone. Penny's voice sounded a little out of breath, like she was running and talking now. I heard a click, then a ding-ding-ding sound, as if she had left her truck door open. "I'm coming. Where are you?"

"We're heading home," I told her. "We'll be there in about an hour."

Roy and Wynter were already on the dogsled. Wynter pulled the brake and River looked back, waiting for a command. I tucked the phone between my ear and shoulder as I hooked myself up to Raven.

"I need you safe," Warden Penny ordered. "Go off-trail, hide in the woods. There are caves all along there. Make a snow fort, whatever . . ."

"There's no hiding with all these dogs," I reminded her. "The minute they hear someone, they'll bark."

"You're right. You're right. I'm not thinking clearly. I'm so worried about you all." The warden swore. She took a deep breath. "Your mothers will be furious with me! Warden Kate, too. I'll be there as soon as I can."

"We'll meet you on the trail," I promised. When the warden didn't respond, I pulled the phone from my ear to check the signal. Two bars. I tried again. "Warden Penny?"

Finally, I heard muffled talking like she'd put the phone down to talk to somebody or was hugging it to herself. "Haven't seen . . . have an emergency now but I can go check after . . . I'll keep my phone on . . . if I hear anything . . . I'm sure . . . " Louder and clearer, her voice came through the phone to me again. "I'm coming, Cooper!"

And the phone went dead.

"She didn't send the plane," I told Packrat. I turned my ringer up as loud as it would go and put the phone in my pocket. "When I told her about it, she sounded scared." One snowflake drifted down, down, down in front of me. Then a second, and a third. The pine tree branches around us lightly danced.

I glanced up at the sky. The predicted snow squalls had arrived.

If Warden Penny didn't send the plane to look for us, then who did?

"Okay, then." I spoke loud and clear to Raven. "Let's go!"

I led the way, Packrat and Summer right behind me with their dogs. Roy and Wynter kept pace behind us on the sled, about twenty feet back.

Right pole down, left foot slide, left pole down, right foot slide, right pole down, left foot slide, and over and over and over to a rhythm in my head. "Hike, hike!" I called to Raven.

Another hour later and we came out of the woods into the clearing with views of Pine Lake. The snow still fell very lightly, so we had an amazing look at the landscape around us. The pine trees, which had dotted the landscape on our way to Piehl Mountain, were now hidden by the snow collecting on their branches.

We stopped for a quick break. Raven sat by my skis, and I patted her shoulder. I ached all over, but my batteries started to recharge just seeing the trail leading to the lake, and the campground beyond it. We were almost there.

I tapped both of my poles onto the trail beside me. "Ready to go down—"

"Cooper!" Packrat handed me the binoculars he'd been looking through. "Look!"

Coming along the trail behind us from Piehl Mountain was a fast-moving yellow dot.

"How many yellow snowmobiles could there be?" I muttered.

"That poacher must want our lynx pretty badly." Summer's voice held a touch of worry.

"And the pelts," I reminded her.

"Wait, what?" Packrat put his hand on top of my hat and turned my head toward Pine Lake and the campground. "This is what I wanted to show you!"

From the middle of the lake, a dogsled team raced toward us. And the musher was Lisa!

I looked at Wynter, her face white as snow.

"I thought she ordered you home. Why is your mom coming this way?"

"It's not what you think," she whispered. But I noticed her quick glance into her basket.

What the heck? Why did everyone in the world want this lynx?

We all looked right, toward the poacher and his yellow snowmobile. Then left, toward Lisa.

I fisted my hands over my poles. "If we move fast, we can make the fork in the trail at the giant rock," I told them. "If we take a right, we can cross the old bridge. They'd never suspect us of going the long way. We'll get to the other side of the lake and travel home through the woods on its edge with the pine trees as our cover. Lisa and Scott will meet up on the trail and wonder why neither one saw us. By then, we'll be home."

We all looked to Wynter. "I'm with you," she said firmly.

Packrat pulled his hat down over his ears. "Let's go!"

We traveled as fast as we dared, heading down the other side of the hill. Would we make it to the fork and get off this trail before they caught up?

I had no idea. But I knew two things. One, I couldn't let them take the little lynx. The pelts, sure! Poaching was bad enough, but taking advantage of an animal that was an obvious pet? C'mon! And two, I had to keep my friends safe. I'd talked them into this. I had to get them out of it.

"Hike, hike!"

Reaching the fork in the road by the giant rock, we stopped.

"Last chance," I said, looking at each of my friends. "If we stay left, it's safer, but we'll run into—"

"My mom." Wynter lifted her chin. "I can't tell you why, but we need to cross the bridge and let her meet up with Scott. Believe it or not, it's safer all around."

A low droning sound reached our ears from the right.

"He's close." Packrat eyes scanned the trail behind us.

"We don't have a choice," Roy said.

"Let's go!" Wynter called to the dogs.

Ten minutes later, we faced the suspension bridge.

Below, the river ran swiftly. Wavy bands of ice lined the edges. The rushing water, pounding over and against large rocks, kept the river from freezing over completely. Just beyond the bridge, the water rushed over a small waterfall and spilled into the lake.

Our town historical society said that at one time, the bridge had been sturdy enough for cars to cross over. Facing it with the dogsled, I had a hard time believing it. The bridge seemed ricketier than I remembered. The cables running across the river above and below the bridge were rusty and frayed in spots. The ropes winding around them to make the V-shaped sides were also frayed. Floorboards were missing, some were cracked, and a few hung by threads.

We stood staring at it.

Even the dogs had gone quiet.

Everyone looked to me. "So, what if we unhook the dogs and let them cross one by one? We can pull the sled across ourselves with the pelts inside. Someone can carry the lynx in its cage."

Wynter nodded. "This way, if something happens to the bridge," she paused to gulp, "the dogs aren't attached to each other or the sled."

"It's my idea," I suggested. "I'll go first."

Roy held up a hand and shook his head. "Someone needs to be on the other side to collect the dogs when you let them go."

"And Cooper, you should take the lynx," Packrat suggested, "but you'll need someone to help you carry it."

I rethought my plan. "Okay, then. Roy first, then the dogs. Wynter pulls the sled, then Summer, and then Packrat and me with the lynx. In that order."

Everyone nodded. It seemed as if no one wanted to speak, like when you build a tower out of playing cards and you're afraid to breathe heavily for fear of knocking it down.

I unclipped my skis. "Let's do this."

CHAPTER 33

*Lynx kittens begin to walk when they are between
twenty-four and thirty days old.*

Roy held onto the left cable. Walking carefully, head down, he tested each wooden plank before taking a step. None of us said a word, and I don't know about the others, but I held my breath. The only sounds I heard were the rushing water beneath us and the panting of the dogs. Wynter, Summer, Packrat, and I each held their leads, waiting for Roy's signal. When his feet were on solid ground on the other side, we all breathed a sigh of relief.

The snow fell heavily now.

"There's one spot where three boards are missing," Roy hollered back. "The one after them is rotted, and there's a couple more along the way, but they're easy to spot. Hold the cable, just in case. The dogs will make it—they're lighter than me."

Wynter tucked each dog's lead into their harness, so Roy would have a leash to hold onto when they got to him. One by one the dogs crossed, making it look easy. She left Moose for last.

"C'mon, boy!" Roy called. Moose didn't hesitate. Walking fast, hopping over missing boards, he made it to the other side and launched himself through the pack to Roy. Taking down our friend, Moose then licked his face.

"Hey!" Wynter called over. "Stop playing with the dogs! Make sure you've got hold of them!"

Roy hollered something back we couldn't hear, then we saw a stick flying through the air, and Moose chasing it. Roy stood up and gave us a thumbs-up.

Wynter picked up the three feet of rope at the front of the sled, turned to stand at the edge of the bridge, and hesitated.

Summer stepped forward. "I can help."

"Wait!" Packrat cried. Opening his coat, he pulled out the hunk of thick, light blue climbing rope we'd used to save Summer. "I've got a better idea!" He took the sled's rope from Wynter and began tying the two together with a becket bend knot.

"Yes!" I clapped Packrat on the back. "Way better idea than mine!"

Wynter looked between the two of us. "Mind telling me?"

"Packrat has three hundred feet of rope here," I told her.

"You'll cross with just the rope." Packrat handed her the other end. "Summer can follow you. Then the three of you," Packrat tipped his head toward Roy, "can pull the sled across to the other side."

Wynter's eyes lit up. "That'll work!"

"Go," I told her. "We've gotta hurry."

She picked her way across, Summer following at a safe distance. Packrat and I pushed the sled onto the end of the bridge.

Wynter, Roy, and Summer tugged until the blue rope pulled tight and the sled inched forward. The bridge was easily wide enough to hold it. But was it strong enough?

Foot by foot it traveled. Every now and then, we'd hear a groan. Halfway across, it stopped. Roy, Summer, and Wynter leaned back, pulling with all their might.

The sled was stuck!

"It's the front left runner!" Roy yelled, as the three of them relaxed the rope. Packrat and I could see them talking to each other. Finally, they tried pulling it at an angle.

Crack!

A board broke free, tumbling downward as the sled surged forward several feet. We all ran to the edge just in time to see the board land on a rock below and break into three pieces, sending splinters shooting everywhere. I winced, imagining one of us had fallen instead. The pieces rolled off the rock into the water. There, they bobbed around in the swirling current which pulled them along, shoving them against rocks, ducking them under the water, until they reached the waterfall and disappeared over it.

Roy, Wynter, and Summer pulled the sled faster now. I wondered if we'd made a mistake putting the sled ahead of Packrat and me. Had we weakened the bridge?

When the runners of the sled reached the other side, I told Packrat to go.

"No," he said solemnly. "You can't carry the cage by yourself and still look down at where you're stepping. We'll go together."

He was right. But I'd feel so much better if he already stood safe on the other side. He must have sensed my nervousness, because he added, "I'll take the back, you take the front."

The lynx crouched low, staying still as we lifted the cage, almost as if it could sense the danger. It looked at me through the top of the cage with yellow, thoughtful eyes.

I didn't have time to find my courage—I just had to go.

Cautiously, I put my weight on each board, testing them out like Roy had. But now, the falling snow covered them, so I couldn't tell if they were the rotted ones Roy had warned us about. With my free hand,

I grasped the cable to my left tightly. I had to keep my eyes downward, watching each step, but I tried not to look beyond the boards to the rushing river below. I could hear Packrat's flapping coat and his heavy breathing behind me. "Missing board coming up," I cautioned him.

"You're halfway!" Wynter called.

Already? I looked up and breathed a sigh of relief. I'd made it this far.

Raven nervously danced at the end of the bridge, held back by Summer, who called, "Careful!"

"I'm coming!" I smiled to show them I was all right. Then I remembered. Raven might be worried about me, but Summer was worried about my friend. "Packrat's right behind me!" I added. "I'll get him to you."

I knew Packrat had frozen in place when I couldn't move forward with the cage. I looked over my shoulder. "C'mon!" I urged.

"That's it!" he grumbled. "We need to talk—"

CRACK!

My left foot broke through, dropping into thin air. All of my weight fell on my right knee as it hit the edge of the hole my foot had made. Holding on to the cable with my left hand, I was afraid to move.

"Cooper!" Several voices cried out.

Seeing Packrat still had his hand on the cage, I let my end down gently. My knee throbbed from smacking the next board. Thank goodness it had held! My breaths came deep and fast, and my heart was thumping out of my chest as I saw the water so far below. I scrambled up and out of the hole, then backwards onto a safe spot, and stood back up again.

I shuddered. That was close!

"Don't scare me like that!" Packrat cried. I looked to the other end of the bridge. Roy stood with his hands on either side of his head, Summer was covering her eyes, and Wynter was covering her mouth. I smiled a little at the sight.

"I'm okay!" I hollered over.

Roy shook his head and pointed over mine.

Packrat and I turned. What with falling and all, I hadn't heard Lisa pull up behind us on her dogsled.

"What are you doing?" she cried.

Her eyes traveled across the bridge to find the sled, dogs, and Wynter on the other side. Eyes narrowed, she pointed to me. "You got my daughter to cross this thing? With my sled! And my dogs?" She grabbed a cable and took two steps onto the bridge.

"Stop!" Wynter cried. I felt the bridge sway and turned to find her heading out on the bridge, too. I opened my mouth to tell her to back off, but she hollered first.

"Get off the bridge, Mom, and I will, too. Just go to your little meet-up." Wynter waved a hand dismissively. "We've got it covered here."

Lisa stopped. "You can't be serious."

Wynter crossed a section with two missing boards.

"This bridge can't hold us all!" Lisa cried. When Wynter only crossed her arms for an answer, Lisa backed up. Once she'd stepped off the bridge again, Wynter went back to land as well. Lisa glanced toward the gray sky, as if looking for heavenly answers.

"Cooper." Her eyes leveled on me, her voice commanding. "Bring the lynx here."

I needed to know. "Why?"

Lisa's cheeks turned red, and I knew it wasn't from the cold breeze or the snow falling all around us. "What do you mean, why? I don't have to explain myself to you. Just trust me, and give it to me!"

"I'm not giving this lynx to you, or anyone! Except Warden Kate. She's the only one I trust—"

"Coop?" Wynter's voice was hesitant now. "You should know—"

"Wynter!" Lisa cut her off, then focused on me again. "Warden Kate isn't here." She held out a hand. "I am."

I shook my head.

Lisa checked her phone, then called out, "Wynter, take the dogs and the sled and meet me back at the camp—now. I have to go!"

Wynter shook her head. The dogs yipped and barked and pulled, trying to cross back over to Lisa. They didn't sense the anger flowing between daughter and mother.

"Go do what you gotta do, Mom. I need to stay here and do my own thing."

Lisa let out a groan of frustration so loud, I knew my friends on the other side heard it. Stomping to her sled, she gave us one last angry look.

I held my breath as Wynter's mother pulled her brake.

"Let's go!" she hollered to her team. "Haw, haw!"

And with her last call, Lisa turned her team around and went back the way she'd come.

CHAPTER 34

*Young lynx might stay together after they leave
their mother. They travel and hunt as a team
for weeks, or months.*

I swung around to check on Wynter.

What the heck? What kind of mother leaves her kid behind in such a dangerous situation? In *any* situation!

Wynter's mouth hung open in disbelief. She stood there, motionless.

Summer put a hand on her arm and murmured something, but Wynter shook her off. Lifting her chin, she nodded to me.

I'd only taken ten more steps when the roar of another motor reached my ears. I looked back to find a blue ATV. Karl! What the heck?

Taking off his helmet, Karl race-walked to the bridge.

"Thank goodness I found you!" he cried. It took three seconds for his eyes to land on the cage. His eyebrows shot to the top of his forehead. "What are you doing?" His voice shifted and he spoke to us as if we were scared rabbits. "Your mother is worried sick, Cooper."

More roaring sounds, and then Warden Penny pulled up on her snowmobile, a Maine Warden Service logo on the hood.

Karl didn't even glance her way. Taking a couple of steps toward the bridge, he put out his hand in an I-mean-you-no-harm kind of way. "What's in the cage? My lynx?"

"*Your* lynx?" I spat out. "It's not your lynx! It's nobody's lynx! This lynx should go free!"

Warden Penny stepped up beside Karl. "Cooper, let me handle this." Turning toward Karl, she asked, "Where did you come from? Are you stalking these kids?"

"What?" He took a step back. "No! They were missing! And I remembered they talked about Piehl Mountain, and some guy had asked me questions about the lynx at the dogsled rides and I got to thinking . . . I became worried . . ."

Warden Penny turned back to me. "I'm here now. Bring the kitten in, Cooper. Then we'll sort out Karl."

I hesitated. Shaking off a nagging feeling, I took a step toward her. "Okay . . ."

The loud, whining roar of yet another snowmobile drowned out the rest of my words. A yellow blur shot out of the woods toward the bridge, making Karl and the warden run for cover in opposite directions. Doing a 180-degree turn, it sprayed snow everywhere before stopping where they'd once stood. Thomas Scott jumped off, throwing his helmet down.

"Hey, kid," he sneered, storming toward me on the bridge. "You got something of mine!"

"Why don't we just throw a party!" I muttered to Packrat. The two of us kept inching backward, side by side, looking over our shoulders before every step. No way was I crossing over to Penny now.

"It's not your lynx!" Karl ran after Scott, grabbed his arm, and turned him so they were face-to-face. "It's mine!"

Packrat whispered, "Wynter's hooking up her dogs. Distract those guys, but keep moving backward!"

"We have your pelts, too!" I spat at Scott. Having Warden Penny here made me braver than I probably would have been otherwise.

"You little—"

Suddenly, Warden Penny had the poacher's hands behind his back so fast, he didn't have time to blink. Handcuffing him in a split second, she tugged him backwards toward his sled and handcuffed him to the handlebar. "Those pelts are evidence, Cooper," she said over her shoulder. "Keep them safe."

I nodded.

The screaming, sputtering, swearing illegal poacher had been taken out of the picture. But what about Karl?

"You can come back now," Warden Penny said.

I gave her a quick shake of my head. I had more questions.

"First, I want to know why Karl had a camouflage suit in his camper. And why he put a blind in the woods." I took a few tiny steps backward.

Warden Penny turned to him. "Is this true?"

"Yes!" Karl cried. "But only because I needed to catch the kitten before her injuries got any worse!"

Summer, Wynter, Packrat, Roy, and I all started yelling at once about how the lynx wasn't his, and how it'd been hurt on the wire in the stupid illegal trap. Karl shouted over us that the lynx was his, while Thomas Scott joined in the chaos by yelling about all the money we'd cost him.

"Enough!" Warden Penny threw her hands in the air. Taking Karl's arm, she walked him to his ATV and handcuffed him to it.

"Wait, what are you doing?" He pulled and pulled on the handcuff, like he couldn't believe she'd actually done it.

"Until I sort this all out, you'll stay there!" Warden Penny told him. "I need the kids to come in. That bridge isn't safe."

The snow was falling heavily now. The daylight had gotten grayer, telling me we were nearing suppertime. Would Mom be worried enough to try to contact Warden Kate?

I backed up another step, and my foot slid a bit. The snow was making everything harder!

"I didn't do anything!" Karl's voice was panicky now, and I heard the rattle of his handcuffs. "I'm just here to bring Cooper and the kids home and to save Lotti!"

I looked up. "Lotti?" For the first time, I heard the lynx in the cage softly mewing.

Lotti.

My lynx.

Everything I'd believed about Karl was suddenly crashing on the rocks and breaking open.

CRACK!!

Both my feet fell through the bridge. For a second, I felt weightless, then my stomach twisted at the sharp drop. I let go of my end of the lynx cage and stretched out my arms. I came to a sudden stop, sharp pain shooting through my arms at the impact. Hanging from the floorboards by my armpits, I grabbed for anything within reach.

"Coop! Cooper!" My name came from all sides of the bridge. Frantic calls. Pleading. Directions.

The warden hollered for everyone to stay put and keep calm. Packrat set down his end of the lynx cage, falling forward on his stomach to grab my right arm. He glanced at a coat pocket with a piece of rope sticking out.

"Don't let go!" I cried. My legs and hips swayed in thin air. With my left hand, I had gotten ahold of a frayed rope between the wooden slats. How long would it hold me?

How long could my friend hold me?

Packrat now had both hands on my upper right arm. "I'll pull you up!" He tugged, slid back on the thin coating of snow and tugged some more, but I didn't budge. Too much of my weight hung below the bridge for him to be able to lift me out.

I tried to push up with my elbows, but I was in such an awkward position! I felt myself slip a little more through the hole.

Two black boots appeared in front of my nose.

"Yes!" Packrat looked up over my head to Warden Penny. "Help me pull him up!"

I dropped a few more inches. My stomach rolled; my head reeled. The rope had pulled away from the slat! I caught my breath. My hand tingled and my arm muscles burned from trying to hold on.

I looked up at the warden.

Warden Penny looked down at me, picked up the lynx cage, turned around, and walked away.

CHAPTER 35

The name lynx comes from Middle English and means light or brightness. It probably got the name for its bright yellow eyes.

"Warden Penny?" Packrat's voice sounded confused. "Help!"

What the heck? Had all the adults gone crazy?

The bridge swayed, making my legs swing wildly in the air. My elbows were on the boards, one hand gripping the frayed rope. My shoulders burned; my lower half felt weightless. My boots, like anchors. I tried not to look down at the frigid rushing water as it rolled over the rocks.

"Stop!" Packrat cried. "Stop shaking the bridge!"

The swaying stopped. I heard my friends on land talking in earnest, as Warden Penny walked away from Packrat and me.

No. No warden would do what she had done!

Karl pulled at his handcuffs, trying to get free, while Thomas Scott laughed. "Unhook me! We can get back to business now," he called to Warden Penny as her feet hit solid land again.

At his words, it got so silent, I could hear the rushing water below.

Warden Penny was the original buyer! The one he was double-crossing with Lisa.

"Really?" The warden stopped in her tracks, inches from the end of the bridge. Her voice was now an evil sneer. "I gave you—*gave you*—this lynx, all wrapped up in a bow! And you let it get away! Worse yet, you got yourself caught! That made Kate look deeper into everything! She's no dummy. She'll eventually figure out I'm involved in all of that, and more. Unless she doesn't come back from the wild goose chase I led her on."

I gasped. *Warden Kate!*

Suddenly, Summer's whisper came from behind. "Hold on!" she said, stepping carefully around Packrat.

She'd brought the light blue rope!

"Roy wanted to be the one to save you, but I need to do it. I won't let you fall," she reassured me as she bent to wrap the rope around my back, under my armpits, and across my chest.

"I planned to go through with *my* end of our deal for the pelts before I disappeared." Warden Penny's voice came across the bridge. Her face screwed up in anger, she thrust a finger in Scott's face. "But not you! *You* broke our deal! You couldn't just trust me even after I got you out of jail! And you offered everything to someone else, because you got greedy!" She stamped her foot. "It's *your* fault my cover is blown. Now I've got to start from scratch somewhere else. This lynx is my ticket out of here. You can stay there, watch the kid drop, and rot alongside your precious snowmobile for all I care."

Scott started negotiating while Karl begged her to let him go, so he could help me.

The bridge creaked and groaned as Summer worked the rope around me. Wynter and Roy called out encouragement to her from the other end.

A huge shot of pain burst through my left elbow and up to my shoulder from having all my weight on it for so long. I gasped, automatically shifting to try to ease it. Instead, my body slid down inside my coat. Packrat's hold on it wasn't helping anymore! Only my grip on the frayed rope was keeping me up.

Summer didn't miss a beat. She knotted the blue rope and took a handful of it above the knot. "Grab hold, Packrat!" she cried. He sat behind her and wrapped a hunk around his hands.

"Got him!" Summer cried.

"Fetch!" Roy called back.

Fetch?

A white snowball lobbed over us and hit Warden Penny square in the back. Then another! The bridge shook as the warden turned. A brown blur flew by us, leaping over me, Packrat, and Summer as if we weren't even there, paws barely skimming the bridge.

Moose!

That big, awesome, goofy dog launched his body at Warden Penny, knocking her to the ground and planting himself on top of her.

"Good dog!" Roy called.

Next to the warden, the lynx cage lay on its side, the door open.

"Get the lynx!" I urged Summer.

"Trust me!" Summer threw my own words back at me. Words I'd used to calm her when she'd fallen through the ice. "We save you first. Then the lynx!"

"Let's go!" Packrat called.

"Let's go!" Wynter echoed.

The rope tightened, pulling me toward Roy and Wynter's side of the bridge. A board under my armpit ripped through my jacket and snagged, jerking me to the left. Then, with a crack, the board broke free and fell. I dropped, dragging my friends across the bridge as they tried to stop my downward fall.

"Hold on!" Packrat cried.

Summer hollered, "Pull!"

The rope jerked, then tightened. I slid up a few inches. Then a few more. Packrat and Summer grabbed my arms, the rope doing most of the work now. When my hips were out of the hole, they dragged me to a safe spot and I collapsed on the wooden planks, panting.

Summer put out a hand to help me up, looking me over with worried eyes. "Don't move yet," she cautioned. "You might get dizzy or—"

"Warden Penny!" I tugged at the rope around me, trying to get free of its knot. "We've got to go after her! She's got the lost lynx!"

"Look," Packrat said. I kept fumbling with the knot, and he said again, "Cooper! Look!"

Warden Penny lay on the ground, Moose sprawled across her, lapping her face. And there, standing over her, was Lisa. Wynter's mom calmly shooed Moose away, flipped the warden over, bent to handcuff her, then helped her stand.

What the heck? If that wasn't confusing enough, I saw Warden Kate, too. She was here—standing at the end of the bridge! I didn't see another vehicle. Lisa must have brought her on the dogsled. Wait! *She* was Lisa's meet-up? Lisa and Warden Kate were working together?

Lifting an eyebrow, Warden Kate put her hands on her hips and stared me down.

"I thought I told you all to stay put! I even called you this morning when Lisa suspected you were up to something."

"You said you needed me," I said hesitantly, walking toward her.

"The rest of that broken sentence was *to stay put.*"

Oh, boy. We had some explaining to do.

"Cooper?" Warden Kate lifted an eyebrow. "I had to use the plane to find you."

I winced. We had days and days of explaining ahead of us. Using a plane to find missing people wasn't taken lightly.

Lisa headed toward Karl, but Thomas Scott grabbed her arm and pulled her over to him. "I know you! You were on the other end of the phone! You were going to buy—"

Lisa shook him off. "Save it. I'm an undercover police officer with the Royal Canadian Mounted Police. You've been caught with enough proof to put you away for quite a while."

Scott recoiled as if she'd slugged him.

Moving to Karl, she released him from the handcuffs.

"Wait! No!" I hollered. "He's—"

The lynx jumped from its cage into Karl's waiting arms—and snuggled close, under his chin.

CHAPTER 36

Lynx den under fallen trees, tree stumps, or piles of rocks.

Karl and Lisa escorted us back to the campground under the light of an almost full moon, while Warden Kate stayed to help the authorities sort out the investigation of Thomas Scott and Warden Penny's poaching and selling of pelts. Warden Kate had kept the lynx kitten, too, so she could get it to a state lynx biologist and have it checked over.

The night sky had cleared, the air felt crisp and cold, and the moon's light reflected off the newly fallen snow to brighten the world around us. It would have been a beautiful trek across the lake if we weren't facing a lot of explanations and our worried parents at the other end.

Lisa took the lead with her sled and four dogs, while Karl followed behind on his ATV. Wynter and Summer rode on the dogsled with five dogs, while Roy, Packrat, and I skijored back. I'm sure Lisa told Karl not to take his eyes off of us for a second, so we didn't make a run for it or something. As if! My armpits burned, my knees and elbows were banged up, and I almost fell asleep twice as Raven pulled me along. I just wanted to crawl into my nice warm bed and sleep for a week.

And I had so very many questions.

Wynter and her mom didn't speak at all until we got back to their campsite. Even though we were tired, hungry, and freezing cold, my friends and I offered to help feed, water, and check over the dogs.

Lisa took off her gloves and rubbed her forehead with the back of her hand. "I think you've all done enough for one day."

Her words hit me square in the gut.

"Mom!" Wynter stepped between us. "That's not fair! I wanted to go. I offered my team. I was worried about the lost lynx kitten and the warden and thought maybe, just maybe, if I helped, you'd look at me differently. Talk to me differently. Let me into your life outside our kennel."

"Wynter! Let you in? You *are* my life!"

Wynter took a step back. "You could have fooled me! You don't talk to me. You don't tell me where you're going when you're on a call. You don't say when you'll be back."

"It's to protect you!" Lisa threw her hands in the air. "If you don't know what I'm doing when I'm on duty, where I'm going, who I'm arresting and why, then you can't worry."

"Not knowing you'd gone from vacation mode to undercover mode is what made everything here worse!" Wynter sighed.

"I had no idea I'd find a lead here, of all places. Warden Kate and I needed each other to solve it."

"That's what I'm talking about!" Wynter's hands went to her hips. "If you'd just let me know, none of this would have happened. Then, when I talked to you on Thomas Scott's phone, you said—"

"I said 'Don't give me away. Don't give up my cover as the pelt buyer until I say so.'" Lisa sighed. "I needed you to listen to me so Scott wouldn't know who I was—so he couldn't use you to get to me."

"We already had him tangled up in netting, Mom." Wynter rolled her eyes. "And Roy took away his knife. I trusted you when you left me to go get Warden Kate from the plane, so she could help. I need you to start trusting me back."

Lisa just shook her head in frustration.

Wynter tipped her head toward us and said softly, "I wanted to tell you all so many times . . ."

Lisa put a hand on Wynter's arm and glared at us. "My daughter and I have a lot to talk about. She'll see you tomorrow."

Summer, Packrat, Roy, and I started walking away.

Lisa cleared her throat. We turned back. "I do appreciate your offer to help with the dogs, though," she said.

Wynter's sad eyes met mine as the dogs danced around her, waiting for their supper and bed. We nodded at each other.

Roy, Summer, Packrat, and I didn't say a word as we walked toward the well-lit office where all our parents waited.

As we stepped onto the porch, a figure walked out of the shadows.

"Cooper."

Karl stood before us. Hands deep in his pockets, his shoulders hunched, he looked like he'd been trampled by a herd of deer.

Good.

"Can I talk to you? All of you?"

I wanted to yell at him, tell him what I thought of him, push by him and leave him there. But I wanted answers more.

I simply asked, "Why?"

"You were right. I wanted a new mascot." Karl leaned against the porch railing. "When I had Petunia, I had so many requests in New England to give my wildlife talks, I had to say no to some each year. Without her," he shrugged sadly, "I was lucky to get asked ten times a year. That didn't cover my bills.

"So, I went online and fell in love with a lynx kitten. The breeder assured me she was hand-raised, house-trained, and affectionate. So, I sent in my permit to import her to Vermont, own her, and exhibit her in educational presentations. I knew the permit would take time. Vermont Fish and Wildlife doesn't issue these permits without checking everything over—me, my house, the animal's habitat. Besides, I needed someone to build an enclosure attached to the house so Lotti could have outdoor space.

"So, I asked the breeder to hold her for me until I could set everything up. He refused. He told me only one lynx remained, and another offer had come in." Karl ducked his head. "It should have been a red flag to me that something was fishy. Instead, I drove to North Carolina that day."

"So, you have the permit now?" Summer asked.

Karl shook his head. "No. It's taking longer than I thought. Because I'd had a permit before, I'd figured I could get one for the lynx with no problem. I was wrong."

"You knew you needed a permit to bring her into Maine, too?" I asked.

"How could I get a permit to bring her here, when I didn't even have the permit to own her yet?" Karl's eyes begged for my understanding. "I knew within a couple of days of getting her home that she wasn't hand-raised. Lotti sat in the window and cried. She went to the bathroom all over the house and didn't use her litter box. She didn't eat well. She tore apart my furniture. I called the breeder, but the number had been disconnected. After a lot of digging, I found out they weren't true breeders. They'd ripped Lotti from her den and family at twenty weeks old."

"You knew all that, and yet you planned to take a wild lynx to your library presentations here?" I spat out the words. I couldn't believe he'd take such a risk with people. Or the lynx!

"No!" Karl put up a hand. "Absolutely not. The only reason I brought her is because I didn't have anyone I could trust to watch her. She'd gotten so big these last couple of months! My plan was for her to stay in her crate, and I'd walk her on a leash when no one was looking. I just needed the money." His voice trailed off.

"So the first time we brought you wood and water . . ." Packrat began.

"She'd already escaped," Roy said.

Packrat crossed his arms. "Why didn't you just tell us?"

"Because there's a big fine if you lose your exotic pet."

My steely gaze locked on Karl. "So it's all about the money."

Karl looked ashamed. "I . . . I almost confessed at the campfire, back at the beginning of the week. But . . ." Karl ran his hand over the top of his head. "Well, yes, I thought about the fine. But you also gave a passionate speech, Cooper, on why wild animals should stay wild. I didn't want to disappoint you with my actions."

I remembered my speech. And I remembered his response: *Owners of pets have an obligation to care for them the best they can for as long as that animal lives, exotic or not.*

"I hoped to catch her with food, when she got hungry enough," said Karl. "She'd turned her nose up at the specialty food I'd bought for her. But she did come near for the fish. Just not near enough for me to grab her without her collar."

"*You* stole our fish!" Roy sputtered. "A man shouldn't steal another man's catch," he muttered.

"I'm sorry I stooped so low," Karl said, "but I was desperate to feed her. And I wasn't catching fish big enough to keep."

"Does Warden Kate know all this?" I asked.

Karl nodded.

"She's taken my info. I'll get some heavy fines and probably never get a permit for a wildlife mascot again. It won't matter, though." He sighed heavily. "When word of this gets out, I'm sure I won't be asked to give wildlife presentations anymore either."

Karl stepped off the porch.

"I'm packing up. I'll leave at first light. Again, I'm sorry, Cooper. All of you, keep doing what you're doing for the wildlife in your area. They need you."

As we watched Karl walk away, I realized this adventure had two suspects who were truly guilty, and one who was kinda-sorta guilty.

But it also crossed my mind that if Karl hadn't brought the little lynx this week, Warden Penny and Thomas Scott would have made their deal for the pelts, Scott would have gone on poaching, and probably no one would have ever known.

Much later that night, after our parents had hugged us, yelled at us, and hugged us again, Warden Kate showed up to say that Warden Penny and Thomas Scott had been taken away, and this time, neither of them would be released before their trial.

Warden Kate confirmed that Scott had been poaching on and off in the area for a long time. He'd been a ghost in the woods, seeing everything, but not being seen. After he'd collected more than his share of hides, he had sold them to people like Penny, who didn't count and didn't care. People who had connections to get them over the border into Canada and sell them, while keeping Scott's name out of it.

Lisa and Wynter were here on a mini vacation, just as Wynter had told us. But it turned out Lisa had been working on a case in Canada, tracking someone who constantly brought many, many pelts over the border into her country. She and Warden Kate had been working on the same case and didn't know it until their leads intersected here at the campground.

Wynter and Lisa's argument made a little more sense now. So did the gun I had seen in Lisa's coat pocket.

Roy had gone with Packrat and his mom back to their trailer. Stacey sniffled, lectured, then sniffled some more. Summer's dad had simply put his hands on her shoulders, shaken his head, hugged her, and said, "The lengths you'll go to, in order to save an injured or lost animal. We'll talk about this at home."

My mom? Well, she didn't say a word in the office in front of everyone. That's how I knew the level of trouble I was in. It was high.

After the office had cleared out and we'd locked up, Mom and I crossed over to the house. Molly came running into the kitchen, dressed in her pajamas, to hug me, but Mom told Molly to go to bed.

"I want to hear about Cooper's adventure!" she'd argued.

"I need to talk to Cooper alone right now, Molly," Mom said. As she shooed Squirt out of the room, I saw for the first time how tired—no how sick—she was.

Now I felt guiltier than ever.

Mom and I talked for an hour, until neither one of us could keep our eyes open or hold our yawns back. Mostly, she was upset that I hadn't told her where I was going, and why. Let's face it, though; if I'd asked for permission, she wouldn't have let me go at all.

After a lot of back-and-forth, I agreed to a three-week-long grounding, plus whatever Dad tacked on when he got home and heard about our trek.

But she did agree to let the punishment begin after the festival was over.

"You planned the whole week," Mom said, "and we have customers here, so you need to finish it."

I'd never admit it, but I think I got off a little easy.

CHAPTER 37

There are four species of lynx in the world, including the bobcat. They're all hunted for their beautiful fur. For this reason, the Iberian lynx struggles to survive in the mountains of Spain.

I woke up early on the last day of our Winter Festival for three reasons.

One, I couldn't wait to hang out with my friends doing cool winter stuff like racing kayaks across the ice, ice-fishing, sledding, and having a snowball fight.

Two, after today, I'd be grounded for weeks.

And three, Wynter had asked if we could talk over cocoa and muffins in the store.

"I wanted to explain my mom to you, Cooper. She's not a bad person. She just . . . well, she worries about me. A lot."

At my nod to go ahead, she took a deep breath and jumped in.

"When I was eight, I began to notice what my mom's other job was away from the kennel. I bugged her every day for stories about being a police officer. I soaked them up, Cooper, memorized them! Mom is a super storyteller, and I hung on her every word, wanting to be just like her when I grew up.

"One day, though, Mom told me about how she'd chased a suspect, taken a shortcut, and surprised the man by jumping off someone's porch and tackling him when he ran by. The next day, while Mom was working," Wynter said, wincing, "I re-created the chase. I actually climbed out my second-floor bedroom window and jumped onto a leaf-stuffed dummy in a pile of leaves on the ground."

"No way!" I cried. "Ouch!"

"Yeah. Dumb, I know. I broke my leg got a concussion, and was laid up for a long time. Up until yesterday, Mom has refused to tell me any more work stories.

"But it's been seven years!" Wynter complained. "I keep telling her I'm older now. I know not to throw myself off roofs." She and I laughed lightly. "Then, at the start of this school semester, I signed up for a junior warden class. My dream is to combine my love of law enforcement with my love of nature. I didn't tell Mom; I didn't want her to pull me out. But right before we left on this trip, my teacher ran into Mom in the grocery store and bragged about what a natural I am! Oh, did we fight! All that night, into the next day. But I stood my ground, and she was starting to come around, warming up to the idea. Then she meets you all and sees you 'playing at being wardens.' "

I started to protest, but Wynter held up her hand. "Her words, Cooper, not mine. Anyway, that's why she kept me in the dark about everything. About the investigation back home, about her link to it here—about working with Warden Kate, even!" Wynter apologized with her eyes. "Hearing her voice on Thomas Scott's phone was a shock to me, too. If she'd just trusted me, we all could have backed off and let them find the lost lynx. Sorry, Cooper."

"I'm not sorry!" I leaned across the table. "Sure, it would have been easier. But then our great adventure together never would have happened!"

Wynter looked at her watch, then stood to put her mug by the sink.

"You know, Warden Kate had a long talk with my mom about you and your friends. She thinks you'll make a great game warden someday."

I got up and we walked side by side through the store. A hand on the door, Wynter said softly, "I wouldn't be surprised if my mom pulls you aside to apologize, before we go."

We hung out lakeside all day long. Campers who'd heard how we'd found Thomas Scott, saved the lynx kitten, and exposed Penny stopped to congratulate us. We must have told our adventure story a gazillion times!

Packrat, Roy, Summer, and I stood around a bonfire by the lake's edge having our last s'mores of the week. This time, Packrat brought chocolate graham crackers, peanut butter cups, and regular marshmallows. As the sun moved past the noon mark to slip lower and lower in the sky, I felt my free time slipping away, too.

Hearing the swish of dogsled runners, I shaded my eyes to find Wynter and her mom heading toward us from their ride around the lake. Seeing them share a laugh, I smiled, knowing they were working things out the best way they knew how.

On the trail.

"Whoa! Whoooooooa!" Wynter called to Raven and her team.

The dogs stopped, happily wagging their tails and barking in excitement.

I went over to crouch in front of Raven, who was in her lead position. "I'm gonna miss you, girl!"

"Me too?" Wynter asked from behind me.

Standing up, I turned to her. "Maybe someday, we'll find ourselves working on the same case, like Warden Kate and your mom."

Roy, Packrat, and Summer wandered over.

"I'll miss you, too," Packrat said shyly.

"Me, too," Summer said. "You'd better stay in touch. You owe me an overnight under the stars!"

"And what about you?" Wynter looked at Roy from under her lashes and grinned.

Roy's ears turned bright red. He cleared his throat. "Maaayyybe."

Wynter nudged his shoulder with her own. "Me, too. *Maybe* I'll miss you. Sooooo, you get one last guess at my name before I claim you as my human target."

Roy seemed to consider it. Putting his hands in his pockets, he stared at his boots. Finally, he said, "Wynter Borealis."

Wynter's tinkling laugh echoed along the beach front and out onto the ice.

"Really?" I whispered. "*That's* your last guess?"

"What?" As Roy stood tall, I was surprised to find he was a little hurt by our reactions. "It was a solid guess!" Pointing to Wynter he said, "You love Canada. You love camping out under the stars. And you love winter. The season, I mean."

Wynter stilled. She blinked several times. In a soft voice, she said, "Roy. You've been paying attention."

"Wynter Pearl!" Lisa called from her sled. "We've got a lot of packing to do!"

"Coming, Mom!"

Wynter took three steps toward her sled, turned around, ran back, and kissed Roy on the cheek. "Bull's-eye," she said with a giggle. And then she was gone.

"Looks like she traded one hundred snowballs for one kiss," Summer teased.

My friend stood speechless with a hand on the very spot Wynter had kissed, long after she'd yelled, "Let's go!" to her team.

Packrat gave Roy three heavy pats on the shoulder, congratulating him or sympathizing, I wasn't sure which. Suddenly, like a lightning strike, I realized Roy hadn't been annoyed by Wynter this whole time. He'd *liked*-liked her!

I shot a sideways glance at Summer to find her studying me, too. We both looked away quickly. I cleared my throat. She bit her lip.

"Oh, for heaven's sake!" Packrat looked up at the sky. "If I ever find a girl I like, I promise just to flat out tell her!"

Summer and I stared at him. My ears burned in embarrassment. Packrat rolled his eyes in frustration. Taking my hand, he dragged me over to put it in Summer's.

"Cooper? Summer likes you. Summer, Cooper likes you. Now, can we all just get back to hanging out together?"

Summer giggled softly. My ears heated up.

And just like that, everything felt right again.

CHAPTER 38

Lynx kittens are born with blue eyes; they turn yellow within a few weeks.

One week later, Summer came to my house and my dad drove us to the Whittier Wildlife Center, with Mom and Molly tagging along. Standing in the parking lot, waiting for Packrat and Roy to arrive, I looked up at the clear blue sky and felt the bright sunlight warming my face. I could count on more snowstorms over the next month and a half, yet I could also feel the beginning of the end of winter.

There were three signs that clued me in to the fact our winter season was sliding into spring. One, the sap of the maple trees would run and families I knew would collect it and boil it down into maple syrup. Two, the wetlands would thaw, and little spring peepers would emerge to sing loud, high *peeps!* at dusk. And three, male chickadees would call *fee-bee fee-bee* to find their summer partners.

In a way, Wynter and Roy's name game had been their *fee-bee* call.

I grabbed Summer's hand and squeezed. Our *fee-bee* call? Well, I guess I'd just had a hard time hearing it over my worries about what Packrat might be thinking and feeling.

Summer and I shared a smile. I heard her loud and clear now.

She bumped my shoulder with hers. "Hey, did you ever figure out who held the second flashlight the night the lynx got caught in the trap and Wynter and I were lookouts so you could try to free it?"

Wait! Summer had been a lookout in the woods that night? She hadn't chosen Wynter over us after all! She'd kept us safe from the poacher.

"One of the flashlights was Thomas Scott," I explained. "He was coming up from the lake to check the trap. The other was Warden Penny. But she wasn't there to help Warden Kate; we hadn't even called yet about the lynx. She was there to help Thomas. That was a clue Warden Kate figured out."

Warden Kate's truck pulled into the parking lot. Packrat and his mom were just behind her.

The warden got out of her truck and turned to us with a smile. "Ready?"

"We're just waiting for—" I didn't have to finish. Roy and his dad pulled into the driveway and parked next to the warden. Roy threw open the passenger door and practically flew from the car.

"Wait for me!" he called.

As if we'd do this without him.

The warden was the reason we'd all been let off being grounded for the day. She led us through the wildlife center's gate, then closed it behind us. Like the campground, this place was wall-to-wall people from April to November. But in the winter, the center was closed to human visitors. Larger mammals like fox, moose, and coyotes stayed in their habitats, because, after all, they're used to Maine winters. Smaller mammals and some birds were moved to more protected enclosures. I'd never been here in the winter. It was pretty cool to be the only visitors!

We followed a wide, dirt path through the woods. We passed the Wardens' Memorial and garden, and the closed-up gift shop on our left. To our right was a large, snow-covered picnic area. In another hundred feet, Summer pointed to some deer grazing in their thick woodland habitat off to the left. Packrat poked my arm to point toward a bobcat curiously watching us from its enclosure. The warden directed us to take a left after the fox habitat and there, behind a clear Plexiglas wall, was a large habitat with downed trees and a group of large rocks, forming a cave between them.

Outside the cave, curled up and sleeping in a ray of sunshine, was the little lynx.

There were so many trees and branches inside the enclosure, it took a minute for me to realize that the other three walls and the roof were made of tall, green, chain-link-style walls.

"Did they make all this in a week?" Packrat asked.

"No," Warden Kate said. "Another lynx lived here for quite a while—twenty-one years, I believe."

"A little to the left." Wynter's voice filled the air around us. "Your other left!"

Wynter had made it here? I looked around, only to find Roy with his phone held up to the enclosure and Wynter's face on his small screen.

"Can you see her now?" he asked.

"Yes. Awwwww." Wynter's voice held a tinge of sadness.

"I have to admit," I said to Warden Kate, "I was hoping we'd be watching you release her."

"Sadly, that wasn't possible," said a new voice.

Warden Kate turned to smile at the tall man walking toward us.

"Kids, this is Wayne. He's the park supervisor."

Wayne wore a dark green uniform, and over it, a thick green coat with a tan collar and the Whittier Wildlife Center logo on the pocket.

"I've heard a lot about you," Wayne said, tipping his green ball cap back. He held out a hand to each of us in turn, and then our parents. "Warden Kate asked if I could be here, in case you had any questions about the lynx and her new home here at the center."

As if she knew we were talking about her, the lynx raised her head, stretched her front paws, and yawned so big, we could see her pointy teeth. Opening her eyes, she looked right at us.

"Can't you teach Lotti how to live in the wild?" Packrat asked Wayne. I saw my friend studying the walls of the habitat and I knew he wasn't liking the idea of our lynx in a cage.

"We don't rehabilitate animals here," Wayne explained. "If an animal is placed with us to live out their days, it's because a wildlife rehabilitator decided it wouldn't have much of a chance surviving on its own in the wild."

"What's a rehab . . . rehab—" Molly said, stumbling over the word.

"Rehabilitator," I explained. "You see, when Warden Kate finds an orphaned or injured animal—"

"Or an animal that's owned by humans illegally," Summer added.

"—she takes them to a rehabilitator. They're specially trained to treat wildlife injuries, feed animals, and care for them, all the while hoping to release them back to their native habitat."

"Ah," Roy nodded. "So, they make the call on whether or not an animal could survive on its own."

"I had no idea!" Mom said.

"Sadly, many people leave animals in a box at our gate thinking we're the ones who rehabilitate," Wayne said, "when actually, we're the last resort."

Molly went right up to the glass to study the lynx.

Lotti stretched again, then sat up. Walking over to the downed tree, the kitten jumped up to walk across it.

"So, they can't let her go when she's all grown up?" Molly asked.

I put my arm around her shoulder. "No. This one is too used to humans now. She ate what Karl fed her. The poacher caught her easily. You should have seen her jump into Karl's arms at the bridge and snuggle up to him. She wouldn't survive long out there in the wild."

"What are some of the other animals' stories?" Wynter asked over Roy's phone.

Wayne pushed his ball cap back again. "Well, we have an albino raccoon and a fawn. If they were released, they'd stand out like marshmallows at a campfire to a predator, especially in the summer."

"I once helped transport a two-month-old pair of mountain lion cubs to the center, a brother and sister," Warden Kate told us.

"I remember that!" Wayne said. "Their mother had been hit by a car. And then there's our young, orphaned moose," he said with a sigh.

"I read about him!" Summer told us. "It hung out in somebody's yard, and even made friends with their dog. The mother never came back for it."

Wayne nodded. "You see, moose calves quickly get attached to whoever feeds them."

I turned to Lotti, who was lying on the log now. "At least we know she's safe here."

"Your lynx will get only the best of care from our gamekeepers," Wayne assured us.

"Lotti has a job in return," said Warden Kate. She put a hand on my shoulder. Everyone joined us in watching the lynx kitten. "As people visit the park and see the Maine animals up close and personal, hopefully they'll also take the time to learn about them, and how humans and wildlife can share the land together."

"So, Lotti *will* be a wildlife ambassador after all," I said.

Wayne's radio crackled, and someone said his name.

"I've got to go," he told us. "Apparently, we're getting an orphaned bear cub today, too."

Warden Kate and the adults headed back toward the gate with Molly.

My friends and I lingered for one last look at the lynx.

"Can't put it off any longer," Packrat said, pulling his hat low and tucking his hands deep in his pockets.

Summer sighed. "Yeah. It was nice to get a few hours' break from being grounded."

Reluctantly, we walked away from the lynx habitat.

"I'm sorry," I said to my friends as I kicked a snowball off the path. "Being grounded stinks."

"Don't be sorry," Packrat insisted, putting a hand on my shoulder. "We might be grounded for a couple weeks more—"

"But it was worth it!" Roy finished with a grin. "We caught a poacher and a pelt buyer."

"And saved a lost lynx!" Summer chimed in, her hand finding mine and holding on tight.

I knew I'd miss my friends desperately over the next few weeks.

"With any kind of luck," I said, "when the campground opens again in May, our parents will have forgotten all about this adventure." I grinned. "And we'll be ready and waiting for the next one."

Acknowledgments

In my family's twenty-seven years of owning Poland Spring Campground, we never did open for winter camping. And the closest we came to experiencing it ourselves was when my family lived in a travel trailer through the winter on the camp property, as we built a new home inside the gate.

I remember random experiences from that time: like how our pillows froze to the wall in the middle of the night because of the condensation from our breathing, my poor teenage daughter going without a private bedroom for five months, our cat suddenly opening doors, and adopting our beloved pup, Cookie, in the middle of it all. Most importantly, I remember how living in a small space over those frigid winter weeks made us closer in so many ways.

Working with Allyson Maiolo's Florida classroom during the winter of 2018–19 reminded me that not everyone gets to experience standing on the ice in the middle of a frozen lake, having an epic snowball fight, or waking up to find it's a snow day. Seeing winter through her students' eyes was so much fun! It made me want to write a story for Cooper and Packrat fans to showcase Maine's winter activities and sports. There are so many—way too many for one book. So, I carefully selected the activities Cooper, Packrat, and Roy would love, keeping in mind that I'd need to find one unique activity to be at the heart of this book.

One March day, as I walked a snow-covered all-purpose trail just a few miles from my new home, I spied a pack of dogs in the distance running toward me, fast. Upon second glance, I realized it was a team, pulling a sled! Dogsledding! What struck me most in that moment was how happy the dogs seemed as they pulled their passengers through the snow-covered Maine woods. When they passed me, I immediately envisioned a black-haired teen on the back of the sled, proudly calling to her team, "On by!"

Before I left the trail that day, I introduced myself to Alex Therriault of Ultimate Dog Sledding Experience in Oxford, Maine. He and the rest of his crew were so gracious, answering my questions and introducing me to the dogs. At home, I looked up Alex's website, ultimatedogsleddingexperience.com, and was impressed to discover he'd been dogsled-racing since the age of three.

Alex, I knew right then you were the expert I needed to read *Lost Lynx* for dogsledding accuracy, as you were someone who hadn't let being young hold you back from doing what you love. Just like Cooper. Thank you for taking the time to read Wynter's storyline and advising me on it. I look forward to meeting up with you on the trails again.

In *Lost Lynx*, Warden Kate makes an arrest and launches an investigation. Game wardens face great danger every day, especially when apprehending poachers. I wanted to be sure I portrayed it all accurately, so I asked Sam Stone to be my expert for that storyline. A Poland Spring resident and a former student at the school where I teach, I knew Sam was a lynx lover and wildlife geek, and that being a park ranger/game warden was in his blood. Sound like a certain character you know, dear reader?

Sam, thank you for answering my many, many questions. You remind me of your dad, in the years he was our warden. And thank you, too, for reaching out to Jennifer Vashon, Maine State Black Bear and Canada Lynx Biologist, to help us when you didn't have a ready answer. Your thoughtful critique, and Jennifer's notes on poaching and traps, made this story richer in so many ways. If Cooper, Roy, and Packrat were real, you all would be fast friends.

As always, I need to give a special shout-out to Maine's RSU 16, the district where I teach. Every time a staff member or student reaches out to tell me they've read a book in the series, I'm so pleased and appreciative. I wish I could thank everyone here individually, but I'm afraid I'd forget someone.

Whittier Middle School students figure out pretty easily that I can be distracted from schoolwork with a quick question about my latest project. With *Lost Lynx*, this often led to their own personal tales of ice-skating, snowmobiling, snowshoeing, and other winter adventures. Thank you all so much! Your tips and real-life stories helped round out this book.

A special thank-you to teachers Shannon Shanning, who began planning a book launch for *Lost Lynx* even before I'd finished my second revision; Serrene Gagnon, for being my snowmobiling and ice-fishing expert; and Kim Adler, for her knowledge of arrests, courts, and fines.

The Maine Wildlife Park has long been a favorite wildlife-watching haunt of mine. When we moved to Maine in 1991, it was a small park with only a few Maine animals. Over the years, I've watched it grow by leaps and bounds, adding larger habitats and educational elements, mostly through volunteer work. The Maine Wildlife Park was always my top recommendation when campers asked about local day trips.

While doing research over the last few years, so many of the Wildlife Park gamekeepers helped answer my questions while introducing me to their wildlife ambassadors. Thank you all for your service in caring for our animals that cannot be safely released back into the wild. It's obvious you adore them.

Melissa Kim, I was ecstatic when you agreed to hop on board for another Cooper and Packrat adventure! During the very last round of revisions, my own personal trek became a sudden series of high and low trails, S-curves, and delays. But you guided me through, let me rest when I needed, and kicked me back into gear when it was time. Thank you for being my editor, my cheerleader, and most of all, my friend.

Carl DiRocco, at the time I write this, you've only just finished reading your draft of *Lost Lynx* and have begun to create the illustrations. Thank you for bringing Cooper, Packrat, and their friends to life, time and time again. Whenever you reveal your sketches to me, it feels like Christmas morning! I can't wait to see this story through your eyes.

Lost Lynx wouldn't have been possible without the support of Dean Lunt and the amazing, knowledgeable staff at Islandport Press. Your tireless enthusiasm for Cooper and Packrat, getting their adventures out into the world, means more to me than you'll ever know. Whenever friends and family forward me a picture of the series displayed on a bookstore shelf, I can't help but smile and think of all of you.

Copy Editor Melissa Hayes, thank you for your eagle eye! I always feel better knowing you've had one last look at my manuscripts before we officially say, "The End."

Aunt Ginger (Piehl), I was so lucky to have you as my guide to understanding the B-52 crash site on Elephant Mountain near Greenville, Maine! What a memorable hike; interesting, unique, and sobering. Thank you for leading me to it.

After seeing the memorial, I wanted to create a similar setting in *Lost Lynx*, so my son Ben, who is a pilot, helped me to brainstorm a fictional crash site: the Hercules Crash Site Memorial on Piehl Mountain. And yes, I used my mother's family name of Piehl because I know every one of them would own a whole mountain if they could.

David, Alex, and Ben, I had fun imagining what Poland Spring Campground would have looked like if we'd opened to winter campers. I must admit, though, that through the years I enjoyed having our forty-acre campground all to ourselves in the winter. Snowshoeing our hiking trail during a snowstorm with Cookie leading the way, walking the length of Lower Range Pond on the ice, and sliding down our "big hill" from the game room to Site 90—we made so many winter memories!

I do miss running our campground together as a family, during both on and off-season. I suspect I always will.

About the Author

Tamra Wight lives in Turner, Maine. She and her husband and their two children ran the Poland Spring Campground for twenty-five years. During the school year, she works as a teaching assistant at Whittier Middle School. Between the two, she has more writing inspiration than she knows what to do with! She is the author of *Mystery on Pine Lake*, *Mystery of the Eagle's Nest*, *Mystery of the Missing Fox*, and *Mystery of the Bear Cub*, the first four Cooper and Packrat adventures, as well as *The Three Grumpies* (illustrated by Ross Collins). When Tamra isn't writing, she enjoys wildlife watching, hiking, geocaching, kayaking, power-walking, and snowshoeing. You can see her wildlife photos on her website, www.tamrawight.com.

Other young adult books from Islandport Press

What the Wind Can Tell You
By Sarah Marie A. Jette

Finchosaurus
By Gail Donovan

The Door to January
By Gillian French

The Sugar Mountain Snow Ball
By Elizabeth Atkinson

The Five Stones Trilogy
By G. A. Morgan

Azalea, Unschooled
By Liza Kleinman

Lies in the Dust
By Jakob Crane and Timothy Decker